One Sunday Morning

WILLIAM MORROW

An Imprint of HarperCollins*Publishers*

One Sunday Morning

Amy Ephron

FIRST EDITION

Designed by Stephanie Huntwork

Printed on acid-free paper

Library of Congress Cataloging-in-Publication Data

Ephron, Amy.
    One Sunday morning : a novel / Amy Ephron.— 1st ed.
      p. cm.
    ISBN 0-06-058552-8 (acid-free paper)
      1. Female friendship—Fiction. 2. New York (N.Y.)—Fiction.
    3. Man-woman relationships—Fiction. 4. Secrecy—Fiction.
    I. Title

PS3555.P47O54 2005
813'.54—dc22   2004059200

05 06 07 08 09 WBC/RRD 10 9 8 7 6 5 4 3 2 1

For Alan

I would like to thank Henry Ferris, Owen Laster, Delia Ephron, Anna Jane Hays, and Aimee Peyronnet for their kindness and support.

S he never did understand what it meant to be proper," said Betsy Owen as she turned away from the window in a sweeping motion as though her skirt alone propelled her across the floor. And, there it was, in that one understated sentence, an indictment of all that Lizzie Carswell had ever hoped to be and an acknowledgement that there was a story behind the seemingly innocent act they had all witnessed.

Mary wondered, at the time, if Betsy hadn't commented on it or hadn't commented on it in quite the way she did, if it wouldn't have just passed, subsided, receded, if you will, into a faint glancing moment, one of the things you see and then forget about, rather than something as piercing as a shard of glass that becomes forever imbedded in one's memory, so that every time any one of them would see Lizzie Carswell after that, they would remember that morning when they saw her coming out of the Gramercy Park Hotel.

A light rain was falling. Mary Nell felt the soft mist on her face, barely an antidote to the piercing hangover she had from the night before and Billy Holmes' party at the Waldorf that she'd stayed at much too long. She'd had to come in the back door and shut it softly, slip her heels off before she hit the tiled entranceway, and tiptoe up the stairs, so as not to wake anyone. Mama would have given her a lecture that she'd "gone wild" again. Papa would have waited until morning and sat her down over coffee and questioned whether she was chasing something that didn't exist, trying to fill a void, suggested that perhaps she should do something useful, not understanding, at all, that it was useful to sit up late at the Waldorf, to dance, to discuss Kant and whether Elizabeth Harkness' dress was too demure for the season. And, so, she'd had to continue the charade that she was well-rested and obedient, and get out of bed, even though she'd had barely four hours' sleep—it was so hard to settle down after you'd been dancing—her head feeling like damp cotton, and honor the obligation she'd made to go to Betsy Owen's house for a bridge party at eleven a.m. on Sunday.

There would be strong coffee with cream and tea sandwiches, no matter what time of day one visited Betsy Owen, she always served tea sandwiches (as if it was a fashion), and it would be as dull as dry toast. At least, that's what Mary thought, as she turned onto Gramercy Park and stood outside Betsy Owen's brownstone, for a moment, before going in.

There was a family walking out of the Gramercy Park Hotel wearing unseasonable pastels, the mother holding one of those pamphlets that pegged them instantly as tourists. Mary envied them. What it must be like to see New York with a sense of wonder, as an outsider. She remembered her mother taking her to see the Statue of Liberty when she was a little girl and the gift shop that was under the Statue's skirt. She remembered how small she thought the Statue was from the ferry and how big it seemed to her when she was inside the skirt. She still had, on her dresser, the tiny replica of the Statue of Liberty her mother had bought for her that day.

She did hope she would be able to convince her father to let her go to Europe in the spring. She wanted to be in Paris where everything didn't seem so insular, where it seemed it would be easier to write verse, where everyone, even the shopgirls, wore the newest fashions, and, if they didn't, it seemed as though they were creating one of their own, where there was no Prohibition, and the days and the nights seemed to flow into one another, instead of here, where the dark and furtive lure of the night was in direct contrast to the activities of the day.

She rang the bell and waited politely for Betsy to answer the door. Perhaps she could get Betsy to intercede for her with her parents. She could be so convincing. Betsy believed that life experience was worth everything. She wasn't like most of the women Mary knew, not the least bit like Mary's parents' friends. She had an occupation. Betsy was a writer, a celebrated woman of letters, in some circles, and, in others, given a less polite description. She wrote novels about New York with jaggedly exacting prose and minute, if sometimes, recognizable detail.

Betsy answered the door looking markedly older than she had the last time Mary had seen her, as if her age had caught up with her overnight, her gray hair tousled in ringlets like a cap on her head, her eyes still with that mischievous glint that was her trademark, favoring a cane on her left side with a carved ivory handle. She saw the way Mary looked at her—"It's nothing, dear, didn't I tell you? I took a slip on the sidewalk earlier this week. It was silly, really. I turned my left ankle and before I knew it, I'd lost my balance"—she laughed to minimize the effect of the image. "Yes, I know what I must have looked like. The boring part is the doctors are insisting I stay in for much of the day with my leg resting on a pillow, as if it were a poodle." She laughed again, then added, rather wistfully, "They're right. It does swell. But luckily Geoffrey's here and he's been making sure that everyone takes care of me."

"Geoffrey?" Mary didn't know who Geoffrey was.

Betsy didn't answer her. "You are sweet to have come today," said Betsy. "Particularly given whatever you were up to last night." Her voice dropped an octave when she said this last bit. "Whatever it was, I hope it was worthwhile."

"It was." Mary smiled. "Although I stayed too long." Mary hesitated.

She had stayed too long, especially since it was Billy Holmes' party and Billy was fairly soused by 9 o'clock, his bow tie askew and in geometric opposition to the thick horn-rimmed glasses he always wore, and, though he was a cheerful drunk and more convivial as the evening wore on, he had that sense of unfulfilled longing, always, as if he did not want the night to end. He was such an oddball. Clara Hart had startled her by saying, "Have you ever noticed how cute he is?" Billy Holmes! "Haven't you ever noticed his shoulders?" Mary did have to acknowledge that he had shoulders and a certain physicality she'd never noticed before, a bit like a Greek statue, but it was all thrown off by the fact that his bow tie was askew and he had those thick horn-rimmed glasses. It wasn't peculiar that Clara thought he was cute— Clara and Billy had been engaged for some time— but Mary realized that her image of Billy was tied to the way he'd looked when he was ten. How curious to have known someone that long and never noticed what they've grown up to.

"Billy Holmes' party," she said finally. "And it should have been just the same old people but there was the most fascinating man there. He'd been to Nepal—" She stopped because the object of her description walked into the room.

"Mary, I'd like you to meet my nephew Geoffrey Rice. Geoffrey, Mary Nell."

Geoffrey interrupted her. "We've met. Well, we didn't meet exactly. We were at the same gathering last night."

"Yes, we even sat at the same table," said Mary, "but we were never introduced. We talked for the longest time but it was as if we'd missed the moment for a proper introduction or I don't think I ever knew your name…"

Betsy noticed the way they were looking at each other, their eyes locked as if there was no one else in the room. And even though they were including her in the conversation, they seemed to be speaking only to each other.

"Yes, and to think my aunt had told me all about you and there you were sitting across from me and I wondered who you were and I knew who you were all along."

Betsy thought she ought to warn Mary about him but what was she to say? He'd seemed so much better since he'd returned from the East. And she did believe everyone ought to, *deserved to*, have a fresh start.

"You'll be all right, now, won't you Aunt, if I go off for awhile?" he asked.

"Of course, I will," said Betsy, "as long as you promise not to go off too far."

Geoffrey smiled, recognizing that there was a double-meaning to what had just been said. "Miss Nell will take good care of you, I'm sure," he said looking again at Mary. "It was nice to have met you, finally," he said but before Mary could answer, he'd taken his leave.

Lucy Collins had arrived shortly after that and the sedate Iris Ogleby. Lucy was still a bit aflutter from her wedding, the planning of which had gone on so long that even Mary's mother, who never said an unkind word about anyone, had remarked on it. Mary had never understood what was *so* special about a wedding. After all, it was something everyone did, so how could it be *that* special? And what did it matter whether the bride wore white or ivory or how many layers of lace there were on the veil? Or whether there were lilies or orchids in the centerpieces? Why spend all that time planning something that only lasted one day—oh, yes, she knew about the life-time part—but really, just one day for the sake of a memory book? And what did it really matter what the band played as long as you were dancing? (Her father called this her practical side and her mother referred to it as her bohemian side.) But she listened politely to Lucy's recounting of her nuptials to Tony (although Lucy seemed to forget that Mary had actually been in attendance) and their exotic honeymoon on the tropical island of St. Lucia.

Mary would be the first to admit that she disliked (hated, really) the society of women, felt ladies' lunches were a waste of time, would much prefer to be home studying the migratory patterns of birds, or walking on the street observing the people, inventing stories in her mind about their lives, or engaged in a conversation, any conversation, with a man.

The bridge was dull and perfunctory. After the second rubber, Mary took a seat at the window looking down at the Gramercy Park Hotel. The rain had stopped briefly and the sun was just coming through.

"I always like it when it's like this," said Betsy Owen who had joined her at the window, "the moment when the rain stops and the sun starts coming through in patches. It always seems to me as if there's a possibility of rainbows."

And, so, they were both at the window looking out, just at the moment, when a man and a woman exited the Gramercy Park Hotel.

"Isn't that Billy Holmes?" asked Iris Ogleby who had joined them at the window.

"Yes," said Mary. "And Lizzie Carswell!"

And they all saw, as Lizzie stepped into the street and lifted her skirt to avoid a puddle, that she had on her feet, satin dancing slippers, as if she'd never come home from the night before.

"She never did understand what it meant to be proper," said Betsy Owen as she turned away from the window in a sweeping motion, forgetting in that moment all about her injury to her leg. And, there it was, in that one understated sentence, an indictment of all that Lizzie Carswell had ever hoped to be and an acknowledgement that there was a story behind the seemingly innocent act they had all witnessed. And every time any one of them would see Lizzie Carswell after that, they would remember that morning when they saw her coming out of the Gramercy Park Hotel.

As the taxi pulled up to the curb, Lizzie Carswell looked up and saw, across the street at Betsy Owen's house, on the second floor in the window, the shape of two women looking down at her. Was that Mary Nell? She thought she recognized the bob of her hair. Had she seen her? And the wretched Iris Ogleby whose straight blonde hair (which she still wore exactly the same way she had when she was 5) was unmistakable?! Had they both seen her? More than likely, nothing much got past either one of them. Had they seen Billy Holmes?

Seen them leaving the hotel together? Had they seen him put his hand on her back as she stepped out onto the street? What must they have thought? What *could* they have thought? Better not to think about it. She'd never cared much what *anyone* thought. Or, at least, she never let on that she cared. No, that wasn't right. She'd never been in a position to care. Given the circumstances of her early life, her parents separating when she was little, her mother running off like that. *Poor Lizzie. Her mother's abandoned her.* And, the fact that Lizzie was pretty hadn't made it easier, that there was always someone in the room who was jealous of her, even from the time she was a little girl. This part, her mother understood, for, even at her mother's thinnest and most desperate, she was always considered a beauty. "Better to be pretty than not, Lizzie." But she wondered if that was really true. She remembered walking into a restaurant with her mother when she was little and hearing a woman at the table next to them whisper, in a voice so low it seemed almost like a man's. *There's Sophie Carswell. I wondered what had happened to her.* And after her mother left the States, the way other mothers would look at her, with pitying eyes.

Lizzie had learned not to care. She'd learned not to pay any attention. But, she made the mistake of looking up again, just as she was getting into the taxi. Yes, it was Mary Nell, and she saw the recognition and was that something like shock in Mary's eyes. And she wondered if, the next time she walked into a room, she would hear someone whispering about her.

We have to go and tell Clara Hart..."

Lucy had waited on the sidewalk outside Betsy Owen's house for Mary Nell. The rain had stopped but the air was damp still and heavy with the smell of shellfish and garlic from the Italian café on the corner. Lucy wanted to undo the button on the waistband of her skirt. She wondered when the smell of food would no longer bother her (strange to be hungry and queasy at the same time, and the only thing that seemed to help was...over-eating). She tried to figure in her mind when it would be safe to reveal her condition so it wouldn't appear she had been pregnant before she married. But, if she waited too long, she reasoned, the baby might appear to be too early and in fragile health? Perhaps that was the key, to appear to be in fragile health herself toward the end.

She hadn't found the right moment to tell Tony. It had to be a *moment*. She thought he had suspected yesterday morning when she woke and felt his hand lightly on her stomach. He would, of course, know that it was his—he would, of course, remember that—but even he might not want to know that she had been pregnant before they married. She mustn't let anyone find out. Her father would practically disown her. Everyone thought Tony was so successful but he could be such a wasteful thing, with his expensive suits, even his shirts were custom-made, presents for her even when there wasn't an occasion, without her allowance she didn't know what they would do. And her parents fairly doted on her. She'd never had close friends, not the way other girls do. Without her parents, she would be awfully lonely. Why risk a scandal when everything was almost perfect? Where was Mary Nell? Why was she taking so long?

But, just as she began to get impatient, the door to Betsy's brownstone opened and Mary appeared on the doorstep. She watched as Mary took the steps two at a time, her dark curly brown hair cut short, framing her aquiline features, her practically boyish but perfect figure, held straight, as if her walk alone implied how certain she was about everything.

"We have to go and tell Clara Hart," said Lucy.

"I thought we'd all agreed, Lucy, just a moment ago, not to tell anyone, at all."

They had agreed. It had been something they had tossed back and forth. *Did they think it was something that had been going on for a long time? Or was it just a fling? Did they think it was something Lizzie did all the time? It wasn't surprising Lizzie Carswell had turned out that way. Poor Clara Hart.*

Betsy, for her part, would never gossip about anyone again. The last time she'd done it (in print) half of New York hadn't spoken to her for years.

Who were they to ruin Lizzie Carswell's chances? Who were they to bring unhappiness to Billy Holmes' fiancée Clara Hart?

Iris Ogleby believed it was not her place to meddle. She had been raised to that. She believed, in some terrible Calvinist née karmic way, that if you were to strike someone, you would be stricken back.

It wasn't surprising Lizzie had "gone bad", given her mother's behavior. The apple doesn't fall far from the tree and all of that... But who were they to gossip?

But it was fascinating. *Was it truly an affair or just a one-night stand? Was it the sort of thing Lizzie Carswell did all the time?*

Iris Ogleby, for her part, thought it was sort of thrilling if it was something that Lizzie Carswell did all the time since the thought of spending the night with a man was so foreign to her.

Mary Nell had her own feelings on the subject. She had been close to Lizzie Carswell when they were young and she felt, in some way, protective of her. Clara Hart was such a dear thing and she felt, in some way, protective of her. And Billy Holmes had no idea of what was good for him. "I thought we'd agreed," Mary said again, "not to say anything, at all."

"Yes, of course, we did," said Lucy, "in public. In front of Betsy and Iris Ogleby... But if you were Clara, wouldn't you want someone to tell you?"

"Yes, of course, I would. But I have to imagine how Clara might feel. How can we tell her? The wedding invitations have been out for weeks. And, if there is something to tell, isn't it his place to tell her?"

"But if this is what his character is, don't you think we should tell her now, before she's married him?" She took Mary's arm familiarly and began to walk with her down the street before Mary could protest any further.

"But what *are* we going to say to her?" Mary asked when they were only a few blocks away from Clara Hart's.

"We'll soften it," said Lucy. "We'll tell her that we—heard a rumor. You know how rumors are, how they spread, and that we thought we ought to tell her what's being said... And then let her take it up with him."

"And, explain to me again, *why* we have to do this?"

"Because," said Lucy, "if we don't and, years from now, he does something truly awful, we'll always blame ourselves for not telling."

F or Clara Hart, it was a blissfully peaceful Sunday, at first. Outside, the rain was coming down, lightly, almost like mist. Her mother had made biscuits and fried ham and soft-boiled eggs and the smell of fresh coffee brewing had awakened her before she was ready to be quite awake. She'd taken a bath with lilac bath salts, put on a brown gingham dress with sleeves that fell just below the elbow and a dropped waist, and walked quietly downstairs.

Her father had a fire burning in the fireplace in

the study, the smell of pine cones mingled with the smell of cedar wood. He was reading the morning newspaper. The rain beat softly on the leaded glass panes of the windows. Her father didn't notice her, at first. She stood in the doorway and watched him, settled in his leather chair, his soft gray hair thinning, his glasses halfway down his nose, distracted as he always was when he was doing something. Her father was purposefully single-minded. Her mother said that was the difference between men and women, that men were only capable of doing one thing at a time and women, because of their place in nature, were better suited to cook, clean, hold a baby, and carry on a conversation all at once. Clara worried that she might take more after her father than her mother in this regard, preferring to do only one thing at a time. She'd never been that comfortable in chaos. Not that her mother ever cooked and cleaned except on Sundays when both Evelyn and Marguerite had the day off. She could smell the sweet, salty bacon from the kitchen, slightly burned, the way her father liked it. It would only be a few more weeks that she would live here. Strange to think the wedding was three weeks from today.

They had already rented an apartment on 20th Street. It was not the most fashionable of neighborhoods but Billy said that just by their being there, they would set a trend. Clara didn't think there was much trend-setting about her, except Billy. He was attuned to the latest art, music, fashion, nightspots, almost before anyone else, as if he somehow knew what was current a moment before it was. In a way, they were an odd couple. Not that Billy wasn't from old stock, too, but he liked to push at the edges of convention. Even the apartment they had rented was a bit unusual with "an open floor plan"—no wall between the kitchen and the living space. Her mother hadn't quite known what to make of it. Clara had borrowed a bit of furniture from her mother's family house upstate, a love-seat that was pink and so old-fashioned it was amusing and almost trendy, beautiful pewter lamps that she would buy new shades for, three antique French rugs. The windows had been measured and the fabric for the curtains had been purchased and cut. The drapes would be hung next week. Billy's family had given them an old oak dining table and matching chairs, a bit old-fashioned for their taste— Billy had his eye on a Biedermeier but the price was awfully dear and they both agreed they should be careful. Clara had picked the china pattern herself, a simple white Wedgwood, service for twelve, a gift from her Aunt Mae. Her mother had bought the linens, a trousseau of sorts, percale sheets, sensibly cotton, an eiderdown quilt, lace tablecloths, all of which were packed in a trunk and waiting to be moved. It was strange to think that it would only be a few more weeks that she would live here.

"Hi dear, I didn't see you come in."

"Yes, Papa, I know. I didn't want to disturb you."

A moment later they were in the dining room,

warm biscuits and fresh preserves, soft-boiled eggs the way her father liked them, the outside of their breakfast plates scattered with a rasher of ham for flavor and appearance. Clara had barely cracked the shell and let the warm yolk slide into the egg cup when the doorbell rang...

The doorbell rang again, as if someone was leaning on it.

"I'll get it," said Clara. "You two finish breakfast."

Clara's mother Katherine was always pleased when Clara's friends stopped in and knew that she would miss the laughter from the kitchen, the whispered voices, the sound of their feet, as if they were small elephants, on the stairs, but Edward Hart, Clara's father, never liked it when their Sundays were disturbed.

Most likely, it was Mary Nell, thought Clara. Mary had a habit of dropping in unannounced as she seemed to spend most of her time wandering inquisitively about the city. Her father didn't mind Mary Nell so much, thought she had a fairly good head on her shoulders compared to the rest of them, anyway.

Clara was pleased, at first, when she opened the door and Billy was standing on the doorstep. "Hi, Billy."

"Clara..." His voice sounded strange. And on closer inspection, he looked disturbed, disheveled, his shirt was rumpled, his tie askew, his skin ruddy as if he'd had too much to drink the night before. (Of course, he had, she'd been there for much of it. Perhaps she shouldn't have left the party, she should have stayed with him until it was over.) He was still unshaven. He did not quite have the appearance of someone who had come courting.

"Billy, Mama and Papa are still having breakfast.

We got a—late start. Are you all right, Billy? You look pale. Can we go into the library? Would you like some—coffee?" She realized she was talking too much, not giving him a chance to answer. "I'm sure there's still some breakfast, if you want it. Mama's made biscuits. Are you all right, Billy? You look as if you haven't slept, at all? Billy, you're looking at me so strangely."

By the time Mary Nell and Lucy Collins arrived at Clara Hart's house, Billy Holmes had left and Clara was upstairs in her room sobbing.

Clara's father answered the door and explained that he didn't think Clara would see anyone.

When Mary asked if she was ill, he said no, but Clara's mother, who came rushing down the stairs at just this moment, added, "No, but if she carries on this way any longer, I'm certain she will end up ill."

They could hear Clara crying from upstairs.

"Oh, girls. I don't know what happened... One moment we were having a perfectly lovely breakfast, weren't we, Edward? Yes, I know it was two o'clock and all of that, but it is—it was one of our last Sundays together... And the next thing we knew, Clara was sobbing."

Mr. Hart shook his head and retired to the living room, leaving the three women alone in the entrance hall.

"Well, the doorbell rang," said Mrs. Hart, "and Billy was at the door. He's gone, now. Quite gone, I suspect. And she won't come out of her room. I'll ask her, of course, but she says she—doesn't want to see anyone. Did anything happen last night, do you know? At Billy's party? Were you there? Did they have a row? I thought she came home a bit early, given the way you all run wild these days."

Neither of them said a word for a moment and

then, Mary answered quite succinctly, "No, Mrs. Hart, nothing happened, at all. Nothing that we know of."

They could hear Clara sobbing from upstairs even though the door to her bedroom was closed.

"She's terribly upset," said Mrs. Hart. "This may not be the best time. Clara never likes anyone to see her when she's upset."

"Yes, Mrs. Hart, of course," said Mary. "You don't think it might comfort her to see us?"

Mrs. Hart shook her head. "I wish it was as simple as that," she said.

"Will you tell her we stopped by?" said Mary. She took Lucy by the arm and led her to the door. "Tell her—I'll be home until the evening, I'm going to the opera, if she wants me."

Mrs. Hart opened the door for them and they stood and looked at her from the doorstep.

"Are you certain nothing happened last night?" she asked.

"Yes, Mrs. Hart, quite certain," said Mary. "Nothing happened, at all."

Mrs. Hart nodded and shut the door before either of them could say anything more.

won't ask where you've been."

"No, Papa," said Lizzie, "I wouldn't ask that if I were you. I wouldn't tell you, if you did." She gave him a look that was so reminiscent of her mother it was chilling.

"Did you forget, Lizzie, that we have tickets to the opera tonight?"

"No, Papa," she said, changing her tone in an instant, "of course, I didn't forget." She had forgotten completely. "Did you—want to have supper before or after, Papa?"

She hoped he would say "before." She was wretchedly tired and needed something to sustain her. Odds were, they would all be at the opera. Mary's family had a box and Betsy Owen was *always* at the opera. She wondered how many people they might have told by now and if all of New York *was* talking. Billy would probably be there, too. How awkward. She wondered if he would be with Clara. They had not really discussed how they would behave when they next met. They had promised (of course, promised) not to ever say a word about what had occurred but to see each other again in front of so many people and behave as if nothing whatsoever had happened? Lizzie thought that she could manage it, particularly at the opera where everyone was in make-up and over-dressed, but she wondered if he could.

izzie, you've hardly eaten anything, at all."

They'd gone to Tony's, her choice. Her father would have preferred the cloistered booths at the Sherry but it was not conveniently located to the Met. She had ordered the hearts of palm salad, which was strangely bitter, acrid, as if the vinegar had sat too long, and a roasted chicken that had seemed appealing on the menu and less-so on the plate.

Very pale powder and kohl around her eyes, an

egg-shell gown that fell on the bias, framing her tiny waist, she realized that her hands were shaking slightly.

"I know, Papa, I thought I was hungrier than I am." She took a sip of tea. She thought about excusing herself to the ladies' room and, once there, having a sip of vodka from the silver flask she had slipped into the pocket of her coat, but perhaps better to wait until they reached the opera house.

She hesitated, "I've had a letter from Mama. Do you want to hear about it?"

"No."

"Do you want to know where she is?"

"No. The Ashers have just sat down at the table next to us, smile, Lizzie, and pretend that we're not having a row." He spoke softly but firmly, "You know I don't want to hear about your mother. Why would you even ask me?"

"Because I keep hoping that you'll change your mind." After Lizzie said that, she smiled, so the people next to them wouldn't think they were having a row.

"Lizzie, you've hardly eaten anything, at all."

Mary Nell had always loved the opera, ever since she was a little girl and her father had taken her to see *La Bohème*. Mary had been a stand-in as her mother had come down with a cold. Her father used to tease her that that had been her downfall, that her first opera ought to have been *Hansel and Gretel* like a normal 8-year-old, instead of the racy and tragic *La Bohème*.

She remembered the organza dress she wore, and that her father had bought her a pack of lemon drops on the way into the theater, sweet and sour at the same time, with a glaze of sugar. Her father had stopped at the bar in the lobby for a glass of wine. It was before Prohibition and a glass of wine before and in the middle of the opera was considered acceptable behavior.

They had always had the same box, second on the left, off the first balcony, right next to the Meïr-Whites'. The Meïr-Whites were "liberals", at least that was how her mother had explained it to her, Helen Meïr having convinced her husband Stanley White to hyphenate their last names before it was considered fashionable. It was the first time Mary had heard the word "liberal." "Mother, are we liberals?" she had asked. "Yes," her mother answered laughing, "I suppose, in a way, we are but not quite so much as they are."

The Meïr-Whites still looked the same as they had when Mary had first met them and still dressed in much the same way, Helen Meïr-White having never raised the length of her skirt and

Stanley Meïr-White still wearing the same waist-coat, and Mary wondered whether that was an effect of being liberal, too.

She loved the look and the feel of the opera house, the elaborate chandeliers, the smell of the ladies' perfume, the sound of the violins and cellos, dichotic, as if they were considering a skirmish, nervously searching for a perfect pitch before the curtain rose, the massive Romanesque columns, an exact replica of those at La Scala, the gilt-edged molding on the walls, the sense that you were part of an age-old history of theater and that, once the curtain rose, you could be transported or simply daydream.

She was hoping Betsy Owen would be there that night (not because she wanted to see Betsy, she'd had enough of Betsy having spent the afternoon with her), she was hoping Betsy would be escorted by her nephew, Geoffrey Rice.

He interested her. She hadn't been able to stop

thinking about him since she'd met him. He was attractive but it wasn't that. He wasn't like anyone she'd ever met before. He was older than most of her friends. Six or seven years older. He'd enlisted (everyone always said it in whispers) and been sent to France. He had been wounded in the battle of Montfaucon where 27,000 American soldiers were killed. Mary couldn't imagine 27,000 soldiers fighting at one time and that didn't seem to take into account the number of enemy soldiers that must have been involved. It was Napoleonic, primitive, and impossible to comprehend. He had received a surface wound, a bullet grazed his left shoulder. She imagined what it must have been like to lay in the fields among the dying, unable to help them or defend them. And it made a certain sense to her that he had been unable to find his place when he'd returned to his parents' home in Chicago.

There had been an incident which nobody would speak about and, after that, he'd gone on a solitary quest (she imagined, you would call it a quest) to Nepal. When he'd returned, two years later, he had come to live with his aunt, Betsy Owen, in New York. That was all she knew, that was all anyone could tell her, but she knew that she wanted to know more...

There wasn't any sign of him or Betsy Owen in the crowd and, so, she had her eyes trained on the door when Lizzie Carswell and her father entered the opera house and a stillness came across the lobby, not quiet exactly, but it was as if the sound had dropped a number of decibels. A hush had crossed the room the moment Lizzie Carswell entered, and it was clear to Mary Nell that one of them, one of the women at the bridge party, must have already told.

Mrs. Tarkenton was standing next to one of the large pillars in the corner of the lobby speaking to Mrs. Renfrew, and was that Iris Ogleby's mother, by their side? The moment they saw her, they stopped talking. Lizzie smiled and got no acknowledgement in return. She wondered if *this* was what it was like to be cut, then? Perhaps they hadn't recognized her.

Actually, they hadn't stopped talking—Mrs. Tarkenton was adept (a trick she'd learned when she was very young) at speaking without appearing as if her mouth was moving. "Isn't that Lizzie Carswell?" she asked. "She has become a repli-cation of her mother, even down to the tiny waist. I was always jealous of Sophie Carswell's waist."

"Yes," said Mrs. Ogleby, quite under her breath, "and she has begun to behave like her mother, as well, I'm told..." The two women leaned into Mrs. Ogleby to hear more.

Across the lobby, Lizzie felt a chill as if the temperature of the air had changed. It sounded as if everyone in the lobby was speaking in whispers, hushed voices, certain innuendo in the air.

She realized her father wasn't by her side. She didn't have a ticket in her pocket. She wondered if the usher would even let her into the theater.

Old Bob Hatch was staring at her from across the lobby. She'd never liked the way he looked at her, even when she was a little girl, slightly leering, suggestive. She wondered if she could turn and walk out of the opera house without anyone noticing, at all. She'd never cared what anyone thought. She'd learned not to care from the time when she was a little girl. She'd learned not to pay attention to what people said. She could hear them whispering across the lobby. The faces of the people started to blur, become indistinguishable from one another. She felt as if everyone was moving closer, closing her in. She wondered if there was any place for her in New York or whether, like her mother, she, too, would be forced to leave.

And then she felt a hand on her arm.

"Lizzie." It was Mary Nell.

"They're all looking at me, do you see it?"

"Yes, of course, I do. That's a pretty dress you're wearing. Let's just stand here and discuss the fashions of the times. I'm not sure how I'll feel if skirts get shorter. You can wear them. But I think I'd feel half naked. And smile. Smile at me, Lizzie."

Lizzie did as she was told, a feeble impression of a smile but still.

Mary put her hand on Lizzie's arm. "And no one will be able to tell you mind."

Lizzie turned and saw her father looking down at her sternly. "Yes, Papa."

"It's time to go in, don't you think? I hear the orchestra beginning."

She turned back and smiled at Mary Nell. "Thank you."

And then she put her hand in her father's arm—she'd never cared what anyone thought—and walked with him into the theater, as if she had been properly raised to dine and go to the opera with her father.

few hours earlier, they found him, a young
man washed up underneath the Hudson
Street Pier. A shipyard worker named Juan
Carlos Santiago who had walked onto the dock to
have a cigarette was the first to spot him. In a moment of unnecessary valour, Santiago jumped the
side of the dock and slid down a pole (as he explained to the police, he hoped that someone would
do the same for him in a similar situation) but realized, the moment he hit the sand, that it was too
late. The young man was face-down in the water,

lifeless. Juan Carlos Santiago called for the foreman, an Irishman named Kelley, just Kelley (no one knew whether that was his first name or his last), and Kelley had summoned the police.

The young man was wearing a tuxedo. He was barefoot. His glasses had been left on the pier. It appeared he had been in the water for just a few hours. He had no wallet, there was nothing in his pockets except an agate blue St. Christopher on a broken chain. The shipyard workers pegged him for what they thought he was, an uptown sop who'd spent the night slumming. The police could not immediately determine his identity or the cause of death.

It was the talk of Pete's. A young man had been found beneath the pier. It was as if a collective malaise had crossed the room and, with it, a numbing conviction that, though he had not yet been identified, when he was, he would be someone each of them had known.

After the opera, Mary had convinced her father to go home, alone, and had gone, on her own, to Pete's, in the West Village. The hostess, a tiny little girl named Marie with a shock of red hair that fell softly around her shoulders, was the first person to tell her about it. She whispered into Mary's ear, "Did you hear? They found someone— underneath the Hudson Street Pier. He was wearing a tuxedo. Just our age. They don't know who he is, yet. They found his glasses left up on the pier."

Mary couldn't help but think of it. Had they found him late Sunday morning? *Was it Billy Holmes? Could it have been Billy?*

She took a "coffee" (a coffee cup that was really filled with rum) from the bar and took a seat at a table down by the dance floor. She kept watching the door, hoping Billy would come in.

The music was a little too bluesy, a female singer with a voice that wasn't deep enough for the tune, a sad mournful tale about a love gone wrong. One "coffee" and Mary found her way to a taxi and then home.

Her mother had waited up for her. There's a way that mothers can look when they're concerned that can be more frightening than the way they look when they are angry. Her mother had already heard about the young man who had been found beneath the Hudson Street Pier. Betsy Owen had phoned and, when Mary wasn't home, had a long conversation with her mother instead. The police had been to Betsy Owen's house to interview her nephew. *Why would they want to interview Geoffrey Rice?* They wanted to speak to anyone who'd been at Billy Holmes' party.

"Oh, Mama, you don't think that it was Billy Holmes, that it is—Billy, that it *was* Billy that they found...?"

"I don't know. Why would *you* think that?"

"I don't know. It occurred to me the moment that I heard it. Why would the police want to interview everyone who had been at his party? Surely, it can't have been the only black-tie event in New York on a Saturday night."

"He had a matchbook from the Waldorf in his pocket," her mother said. "And—Billy Holmes hasn't been home since early Saturday. I'm sorry, dear. We're all afraid it might be Billy."

Billy Holmes' father was taken to the morgue in the middle of the night by a police captain who drove too fast through deserted city streets in a black Chrysler that Nathan Holmes couldn't help but think was too upscale for the man's position. The city was dark and uninviting. At East 53rd Street, their way was slowed by a milk truck being pulled by two gray horses. In the West Village, a young woman in a beaded dress stepped out into the street unmindful of their approach and they had to swerve to miss her. Two young men were standing

laughing on the corner in evening clothes and
Nathan wanted to roll the window down and
scream at them to go home. The morgue was cold,
damp, with concrete floors, and even when one
spoke in whispers, the sound seemed to echo
through the halls.

The morgue itself was in the basement of the
building, 23 steps down. Billy's father knew because
he counted them. He thought if he held on to pro-
cess, detail, it might obviate some of what he was
feeling. Anger. Remorse. He'd seen where Billy was
heading and hadn't done anything to stop it. He had
written it off to wild oats, the times.

The medical examiner was wearing street clothes
with a white surgical jacket over his shirt. He had a
gold filigreed ring inset with a dark green jade stone
on his left ring finger and Nathan Holmes noticed
that his hands were pudgy and unlined as if they
had been artificially plumped up by too much contact
with formaldehyde. There were only two cadavers,

each lying on a separate concrete slab underneath sheets that were more gray than they were white or else it was just an effect of there being so little light in the room. One was a 73-year-old man who'd been hit by a cab outside his apartment on 102nd Street and Riverside, and the other, the young man who had not yet been identified who had been found beneath the Hudson Street Pier.

It was a terrible moment for Nat Holmes when they lifted the sheet and even stranger when he didn't recognize him. It wasn't Billy. He had so prepared himself for it to be Billy. The relief he felt was accompanied by a strange sense of guilt that he didn't recognize the young man. He ought to have been able to assist them in their identification. It wasn't Billy which begged two questions. Who was the young man who had been found beneath the pier and where was Billy?

Mary Nell was already two steps down the stairs when she heard Geoffrey Rice at the door, asking her mother if she was home. It wasn't yet 9.

"I'm here," she called out. She considered going back in her room, changing her clothes (she'd thoughtlessly thrown on a pair of brown pants and a button-down shirt when she'd awakened), brushing her hair, but she rejected it. "I'll be right down," she said. If he truly was someone she could spend her life with, he ought not to mind what she looked like in the morning.

"Billy Holmes' father was by this morning," he explained, "and asked if I would go and look for Billy and, quite honestly, I haven't a clue where to look and I thought you might go with me?"

"We ought to go look for him," said Mary. "No, I agree. Someone ought to go and look for him." Mary wasn't certain, either, where exactly one would go to look for Billy but since it was Geoffrey Rice who was asking, she would have agreed to go almost anywhere. She looked at her mother for approval. Her mother looked worried. "Yes, I suppose you should go look for him," said Mrs. Nell, "but be careful and let me know how you make out."

He had borrowed his aunt's white Packard which was parked at the curb, and it took only a few moments for Mary to run upstairs and change into a skirt and a more flattering sweater, and collect her coat and they were on their way downtown.

The air was brisk, clean. The skyline of Manhattan framed against a clear blue sky. The cashmere blanket which he placed on her lap for the ride was welcomed but not needed. She studied his profile while he drove. She was embarrassed to admit this—she imagined what he would look like in uniform. Out loud, she said, "I thought Mother was going to die when you implied that I knew the late night scene better than you did."

"That isn't what I implied," said Geoffrey laughing.

"Yes, it is. Turn here. There's a space right in front. There should be someone here, I think."

The Puncheon Grotto was lively. There was still a card game going on in the back room, 5 card stud, the staccato noise of the cards as they hit the table, a clicking sound as one of the players stacked his chips, and behind it, the soft flip of someone shuffling cards. The smell of cigarettes and brandy lingered in the room. Mary marveled at how a place could look so glamorous at night and so shabby in the day and wondered if it was all the effect of electric light and women wearing costume jewelry. Even the mirrors behind the bar seemed dull and lifeless. She stopped to look at her reflection in the mirror. She liked the way she looked in her short-sleeved lamb's wool sweater, her body faintly outlined underneath it, and the way her hair, bobbed, framed the nape of her neck. She looked young, fresh, and as if she didn't belong here, not in the daytime, anyway.

Charlie was sitting alone at a table in the front room, smoking a cigar, and reading the morning edition of the *Herald Tribune*, the business section. Mary thought it ironic that someone who skirted so on the edge of illicit and illegal enterprise would be studying the stock tables but it made a certain sense. It was all commerce.

"I think sometimes, it doesn't really matter what you buy," said Charlie. "Buy ten stocks, half of 'em will go up. Everything's going up anyway. If the elevator man says he's got a tip, he probably does. Who knows who was in the elevator before you. So, why do I read this? Seems like a good way to improve the percentages. Rough night, huh?"

"You could say that," said Mary as she sat down next to him at the table.

Geoffrey added, as he took a seat next to Mary, "Rough couple of nights, depending on who you ask."

Charlie knew about it. He knew that the kid at the morgue wasn't Billy Holmes and that no one knew where Billy was. He had his own theory about the kid. "Out-of-towner. He wasn't one of ours... You see, no one else has turned up missing. No one else has walked in my door this morning looking for their son. And believe me, I'm one of the first places they look."

There was a commotion in the back room, a sound, as if someone had thrown a drink, the shattering of glass. Charlie didn't even excuse himself.

He just got up and walked into the back room. They heard raised voices. Geoffrey put his hand on Mary's back lightly and led her out the door.

Their next stop was Clara Hart's parents' brownstone. Staid, well-appointed, Mary always felt, when she entered the house, that she was walking into Old New York. They reasoned that Clara might know where Billy was. Not that she would give a damn. But she did.

"He's done this before," she said. They were sitting in her living room drinking tea. Clara Hart looked pale, her plain face unadorned with makeup. "He goes off," she said, playing with the silk tassel on a moss-green damask pillow. She caught her hand as if it had a life of its own. "He's not himself when he does it," she said. "It's almost like, I don't know, he gets over-excited and then afterwards, he gets frightened."

"Did it worry you?" asked Mary, sitting upright on the sofa, "I mean, in a real way, about his character?"

Clara laughed, disdainfully. "It did. I guess it doesn't matter so much, anymore, though. I mean, not to me."

Mary was glad that Clara could be a little tough and self-protective.

"I—I might know where he is, though," she said, softly and definitively. "We used to go there, sometimes, to be—alone."

Mary was surprised at this admission, as was Geoffrey Rice. They came as close to exchanging a look as they could without Clara noticing.

"I wouldn't say I want to go with you," said Clara, as she got off the sofa and collected her overcoat from the hall, "but I feel as if I ought to. He might feel better if—" Her voice trailed off and then she added, "I've seen him like this before."

The door to his brother Ned's studio had been unlocked. It was always left unlocked. It was a doorman building, after all, and though his friends all found it comforting that, in a pinch, they always had a place to go, they did tease Ned that he behaved in New York City as if he was living in the country.

Ned was away at a conference. And he had reasoned, with any luck, he would have the place to himself. He thought if he just slept it off, he would feel better. Sleep would help. In any event, he ought not to go home smelling like alcohol. His parents were already on his back about his staying out all night, God knew where! And this time, he might have to agree with them. There were whole patches of the last evening he could not remember, as if they were gaps on a time-line, wrinkles. He knew he had been at the Waldorf and then at Ted's but the method of travel was largely a blank. He remembered, as if he'd gained consciousness while upright, sitting at a table in the backroom at Ted's, a cigarette in his hand that had burned more than halfway down and a glass that was only a third full in front of him, scotch, cognac, he wasn't sure which one, and he could not remember how he had come to be there. No, worse, he could not remember arriving or sitting down at the table. He had spotted Lizzie Carswell across the room leaning against the wall talking to a man he didn't recognize and he was so thrilled to see a familiar face. Lizzie was never judgmental.

He put a hand up to signal her and a moment

later she was by his side, her arms were around his neck and she kissed his cheek from behind. "Hi, Billy, you look a little pale." She took the cigarette from his hand and took a drag and placed it in the ashtray in front of him, a thin plume of smoke dwindled in the air almost like sky-writing. She sat down next to him. There was a young fellow with short-cropped hair, his bow-tie slightly askew, sitting across from him at the table, and Billy felt like he was looking into a mirror at a younger, less-mannered version of himself. Billy seemed to remember that the young man might have come in with him and that he had a funny name like Donnie, that was it, Donnie Wagoner of the Philadelphia Wagoners. He remembered, as if remembering something through a haze, that they had walked over to Ted's together and that Donnie had, in his shirt pocket, cigarettes that weren't cigarettes and they'd smoked one on the way over which might account for why he was having difficulty remembering. His head hurt. Sleep would help.

But, when he lay down to sleep, the room was spinning, as if it was on an axis of its own. Perhaps he should go out and take a walk, get some air, find some coffee somewhere and try to sort out the events of last night which seemed to be choppy, at best.

He remembered Lizzie Carswell coming into the hotel room and a commotion of some sort. Lizzie was never judgmental. But was he the one who had the outburst or was it the young fellow who looked a bit like him? He couldn't remember. He couldn't understand why the young man was wearing an identical bow-tie to his.

He remembered having breakfast, staring down at a plate of eggs, in the restaurant at the Gramercy Park with Lizzie Carswell. She had ordered only coffee which she drank black and stared at him intently as if something serious had occurred. It was something that, if he could remember it, would be an occasion for remorse. He'd gone to Clara's— Oh Lord, why had he done that? He'd gone to Clara's and broken it off. It all had something to do with what he couldn't remember.

Sleep would help. If he could sleep.

C lara didn't say much in the car. She sat in the backseat and remarked, once, on how smoothly it drove, unlike her father's Ford. The ride was slow. They were stopped for the longest time as, in line, two rows of Catholic schoolgirls wearing uniforms, gray skirts and heavy cardigan sweaters with the emblem of the Holy Cross sewn into the front, crossed Fifth Avenue, on their way to Central Park, in the company of four nuns, two in front and two in back, as if the girls were cherished cargo that had to be protected.

The doorman knew her, by name. She took him aside and Mary wasn't certain what she said to him except he nodded and led them to the elevator and took them up to the 5th floor. "It's all right, James. You don't have to wait. We'll be fine."

The carpets were a faded purple in the hallway. The door to Billy's brother's studio was unlocked. It was always left unlocked. Clara hesitated, her hand on the doorknob. Geoffrey put his hand on hers and opened the door for her. She walked in, bravely, none of them knew what they would find. Mary had a terrible moment where she worried that he might not be alone.

Billy was asleep on the sofa.

"We could leave, now," said Mary, giving Clara an out if she wanted one, "and he would never know that we were here."

"No," said Clara, surprising them, yet again, "what would be the fun in that?"

After a moment, Billy opened his eyes and looked up at them.

"You gave us an awful scare," said Mary, her voice harsh, as if she was scolding a child.

But Billy seemed only to see Clara. "Clara, I'm so sorry." She didn't say anything, at first. "Can you forgive me?" Again, she didn't answer him.

He sat up. He'd fallen asleep in his clothes. His shirt was rumpled but he looked strangely innocent. His cheeks were flushed. He made an attempt at straightening his clothes. "Clara, can you forgive me?"

"It doesn't matter if I can or not," said Clara. "You scared your parents half to death. Your father's been down to the morgue."

"Down to the morgue? Why would he do that?"

"A young man was found beneath the Hudson Street Pier," said Geoffrey, "and everyone thought that it was you."

A young man at the Hudson Street Pier. Did he

know anything about that? There were whole parts of the night before that he couldn't remember...

"Clara, can you forgive me?"

"I'm not the one you should apologize to. I'm not in your life anymore. You need to go home and apologize to your mother and father. And anyone else you may have wronged. I don't care anymore."

"Clara, you can't mean that."

Mary felt as if she was witnessing a private moment and that she and Geoffrey ought to leave...

"No, but I do mean that, Billy. You're not in shape for anyone to love you." And she turned and walked away.

"Clara... Clara..." But the only answer was the sound of the apartment door shutting behind her.

And then, he turned and said to Mary, in a moment that said more about his character than anything else, "I suppose, if I want to go after her, I should be better dressed."

Have you heard?" said Iris Ogleby. "Lizzie Carswell has been sent to Europe, Switzerland, I think, to work as an *au pair*."

"How do you know?" said Mary. The news so startled her, she lost count of the cards. It was Sunday again. A month had passed, already a month had gone so quickly, and they had convened for their semi-regular bridge game at Betsy Owen's. It had been on Mary's mind to go and visit Lizzie. Someone ought to visit her. She shouldn't be made to feel estranged, blackballed, as if she was all on her own.

"Mother ran into Lizzie's father yesterday," Iris said, "taking a walk in the rain. Mother thinks *he* ought to take up with someone. That he's turned sour from all those years on his own. He told Mother he's sent Lizzie off, he felt it was for the best. She acted as if she was an independent unit, anyway, she might as well see what it felt like to actually be one. He said she was 'dancing on the edge'. That's the expression he used. He's quite cut her off."

The four women looked at each other. And then Mary blurted out, "One of us must have said something."

"It wasn't me," said Lucy, a little bit too quickly.

Betsy interjected, "How do we know Billy Holmes wasn't indiscreet?"

"We don't," said Mary, "but I wonder if one of us *was* to blame." She looked at Iris. Secretly she wondered if she herself was to blame. She had told her mother some of it, not all, but enough to...

She set the Jack of Hearts down, trump, on Iris's two of spades, and Betsy Owen overplayed it with the Queen. Mary knew she had lost count. Score one for Iris and Betsy.

"I meant to go and visit her," said Mary. "Please, tell me that she hasn't left yet."

"Oh, but she has," said Iris, "she sailed weeks ago on a ship to France. Mother says she bets her father sent her steerage."

"It serves her right," said Lucy Collins.

"Oh, Lucy, you don't mean that," said Mary. Mary tried to imagine what it must be like to be sent off to strangers in Switzerland, with just the clothes in your suitcase and no underlying means of support.

"But—what if she isn't—happy?" asked Mary, realizing, as she said it, that happiness wasn't the point of Mr. Carswell's exercise.

Clara Hart's face was partly covered by a white lace veil as she walked down the aisle on her father's arm. Her dress was plain, elegant, satin with a thin layer of tulle, A-line, cut on the bias, so that her waist looked almost tiny. She had opted not to have a train. Billy Holmes' best man, his brother Ned, looked ruddy cheeked, as if he had already sampled the forbidden French champagne. Billy Holmes looked happy, aristocratic, at home, as if generations of his family (which was true) had been married in this cathedral. His tux was exquisitely tailored but his bow-tie was, as always, askew.

The wedding march was soft, as if it was being played in the distance, led by the organist at St. John's Cathedral, accompanied by an old woman playing a harp. The flower girl was appropriately darling, blonde, angelic, not quite steady on her feet, as if the length of her gown alone might trip her up, but she recovered from her almost stumble with an endearing, mischievous smile. The ring-bearer was solemn, as only a 4-year-old boy with a mission can be solemn, and except for the fact that from behind his shirt was untucked, his suit was, also, perfect.

As the guests were seated, Geoffrey whispered to Mary, "Should any of us stand up and object?"

"On what grounds?" asked Mary.

"That he will inevitably do it again." He took Mary's hand. She was surprised by the action. He'd touched her hair that night in the car, after they'd dropped Billy home, but it was merely to brush a strand of it off her face. He had, once, put his hand on the small of her back when they were walking out of a restaurant but it was only to guide her way to the street. This was, almost, in public. It *was* in public, but no one in the church would probably notice as their eyes were presently directed toward the altar where two people were about to be joined together for, at least, some part of their life. When the strains of the wedding march ended, he made no move to let go of her hand.

It was, by all accounts, a perfect ceremony, mercifully brief, slightly modern (they'd asked the pastor to recite a poem of William Blake's), and certainly pretty, the soft glow of white votive candles burning and baskets of white lilies adorned the stage behind the altar.

Her mother had said to her the night before, "I was frightened when I got married, Clara. I've never confessed this before. You can never know a person's true character or what turns life will take that might change them. You have to learn to take the good with the bad. That's what my mother said to me, 'Marriage has good days and bad days and you have to take the good with the bad.' Not very profound, is it? But that's it, that's all the advice I have for you."

When Billy lifted up her veil to kiss her she said to herself, almost as if it was a mantra, I will always stay by his side.

The wedding party was lavish, a reception at the St. Regis Hotel, why rent a banquet room when one could take over La Maisonette Russe and treat it as if it *was* a private room. There was caviar and scallops and rice with wild mushrooms and grated truffles, and a fancy salad with orange slices and white asparagus. The motif was a reflection of both of their personalities, ice sculptures of Arabian horses, Clara, and the influence of Billy, a big band orchestra that played Dixie and Swing.

One Sunday Morning

Make my bed and light the light,
I'll arrive late tonight
Blackbird bye bye...

There was no division between the two families, as there was at some weddings, with the bride's family on one side of the room and the groom's on the other, in fact, it was downright clannish and hard to tell the Holmes and the Harts apart, the women were all big-boned, with heavy ankles and prominent facial features, as if they had always been related or were cut from the same blue-blood cloth. They all wore simple jewelry, pearls, a brooch or two, nothing garish, and were decidedly backward in their fashion choices, their dresses all an inch or two below the knee. Except for Billy's grandmother, Elsie Holmes, who surprised everyone by coming out in a cloche hat and a fringed and beaded skirt. She was tiny, bird-like, rail-thin, seventy-eight, if she was a day, and she loved to kick up her heels, which she did, to reveal a pale blue garter which she, also, showed to Mary Nell when they were in the Ladies' together and told her it was from "Paree". That was how she pronounced it.

Mary was going to Paris in a week and a half. She had convinced her parents to allow her to accompany Betsy Owen, with the condition that Iris Ogleby go along, as an additional companion. She wondered what was she to do with Iris Ogleby in Paris? Perhaps, Iris would have a transformation in Paris. Not likely but one could always hope... She hadn't told her parents Geoffrey Rice was traveling with them, as well. She had it in her mind, when they discovered it, to feign surprise, and assume they'd known it all along. He *was* Betsy Owen's family, after all. She wondered if her parents suspected that her affections were growing for Geoffrey Rice and, if they did, if they approved of it. Betsy did. She had from the first.

Mary thought that he might try to kiss her to-

night. He had taken her hand in the church and held
it for the longest time. She could tell, by the way he
looked at her, that he wanted to kiss her. It was a
wedding, after all. People did things like that at weddings. Love *was* in the air. But they might have to be
alone for him to try and kiss her and she didn't see
how they would be spending much time alone.

> *No one here can love and understand me*
> *Oh what hard luck stories they all hand me*
> *Make my bed and light the light*
> *I'll arrive late tonight*
> *Blackbird bye bye.*

As the music ended, Billy took Clara's hand and
led her off the dance floor, stopping, briefly, at their
table so that she could kiss her father and mother
good-bye and collect the bridal bouquet. They
looked like the perfect couple.

Shortly after Billy had so unceremoniously broken

it off with Clara, he seemed to realize that he'd made a mistake. At first, she refused to see him. Countless times, her mother had turned him away. But Clara was unaccustomed to the succession of flowers that arrived at her door, a basket of posies on Monday, on Tuesday, pale pink, long-stemmed roses in an etched glass vase, a delicate spring bouquet on Wednesday, tropical lilies on Thursday... Lucy Collins suggested that she turn them away, as well, but Clara said, "What would be the fun in that?" He contrived to be invited to the same gathering as she, a chamber music concert at the Oglebys' which Clara had the sense not to turn up to, as she had been tipped in advance of his intended presence. He lost weight. He couldn't sleep. He exhibited all the signs of a heartsick lover until even her friends began to urge her to see him once, if just to let him down gently. But what none of them suspected, except Mary, was that Clara Hart loved him, madly, without sense or reason, and was cunning enough to know that if she relented too easily, she would not have won.

They did look like the perfect couple, as if they, too, were cut from the same aristocratic cloth. There was a horse and carriage waiting for them outside the hotel, an antic gesture on their part as they were simply going to take a ride around the park and return, as they had taken the wedding suite at the hotel. Iris Ogleby almost knocked Mary Nell down when she jumped up to catch the bouquet and everyone at the wedding had the same thought, that it would be unlikely that Iris Ogleby would be the next to marry.

The wedding party broke up soon after, with-out the bride and groom as a driving pres-ence, there was little left to celebrate. The band-members put their instruments away and smoked one last cigarette at a table in the corner. The waiters, dressed in black pants and white long-sleeved shirts with black silk vests, cleared the last of the dessert plates. Mary's mother had told her, when she was a little girl, that if you slept with a piece of wedding cake under your pillow, you would dream about the man you would marry. Mary suggested to

Iris that she wrap a piece in a napkin and bring it home but Iris, still clutching the wedding bouquet in one hand, surprised her by answering, confidently, "Oh, no. I'm certain that I'll know him when I see him." The guests started to disperse. And, only Billy Holmes' grandmother was left sitting at a table, her legs crossed, her skirt hiked up, swinging her right foot, idly, as if in time to an imaginary tune.

Geoffrey Rice and Mary Nell were almost the last to leave. The streets were practically deserted. The taxis and horse-drawn carriages had all been engaged. They started to walk up Fifth Avenue, crossing to the Park-side of the street. The sky was crystal clear, the stars brightly visible and the moon hanging like a round ball, as if someone had painted it there. Geoffrey had his arm lightly on Mary's back, as they walked leisurely up the street.

"Could you imagine, having a wedding like that?" Geoffrey asked her.

"No, not really," said Mary. "I know that Mama

would expect it. That one is supposed to want it for one's memory book, but it seems like such a fuss for what is, in the end, just one night. Do you think I'm odd about this?"

"No," said Geoffrey, "I don't know if I believe in them, at all."

"In the ceremony or the institution?" asked Mary, surprised that she could be so calm about this admission, if the answer was the latter.

"In either, I suppose," said Geoffrey. "It's all right for some people, who know they want to come home each night, who don't feel they're going to drift..."

"Drift?"

"Go off somewhere without a clear plan."

"Is that what you did when you went off to Nepal?" asked Mary.

"No, I wasn't drifting then, although there were some in the family who thought that I was. I had a purpose. Betsy says I was—" he hesitated. He said this next slowly. "She said I was searching for an evenness of spirit, which is such a spiritual thought it hardly sounds as if it could have come from her, but she's right. I was."

"Did you find it there?"

"No. Not there." He looked at her intently. He put his hand under her chin. He smiled, ever so slightly, just slightly enough for it to be charming and somehow boyish. He stroked her cheek, softly. "I've always wished I could be like you, so clear about everything." He leaned in and kissed her, softly at first and then harder, one hand on the small of her back, the other lightly on her cheek pulling her closer to him. It went on for the longest time.

Maybe it was the effect of the wine or that she hadn't had much to eat at the reception but she felt faint, as if it was hard to catch her breath. No, it wasn't that. It was just that all she wanted was for him to kiss her again. But instead he took her hand and started to walk quickly up Fifth Avenue.

Mary Nell's family's home would not be considered grand, not by J. P. Morgan Fifth Avenue standards. But it was a single family home on East 73rd Street between Lexington and Third. It was an easy walk, as they were already at 70th and Fifth. But the cross strap on Mary's right shoe was starting to chafe. She didn't want to ask him to slow down, frightened he might misinterpret her meaning, as if she didn't want the night to end. Better if he didn't think that.

They stood on the sidewalk outside her house for a moment. It reminded Geoffrey of his family's home in Chicago, not grand, exactly, but affluent and solid. It reminded him of what he'd left. He took her hand. He thanked her. He told her that he'd had a lovely time, that he hadn't expected to. She smiled. He said, "I didn't expect it to be other than an obligation." She let go of his hand so that he wouldn't feel obliged to kiss her again and she wouldn't feel awkward if he didn't try. She said good night and ran lightly up the stairs, even though the strap on her shoe was chafing terribly. When she reached the front door, she turned back and he was still standing on the sidewalk watching her. He had a curious expression on his face that she couldn't quite interpret. She let herself into the cloistered, tiled entryway of her parents' home and slipped her shoes off so that she would not wake them when she tiptoed up the stairs.

First, we're going to Paris. And then Nice. And then Betsy has it in her mind to go to Monte Carlo. I've never gambled. Have you? And then Geoffrey says, if we could manage it, we should try to take a train to Florence. But I'm talking too much and I'm not getting enough done."

"It must feel as if you're going on a grand adventure," said Lucy, wistfully, as she lay on Mary's bed and watched her pack. It seemed to Lucy as if everything was backwards. She should be the one who was packing. Out loud, she added, mournfully, "I wish that I was—free to go."

"But I don't see why I need four pairs of pajamas," said Mary, "and two nightdresses and long underwear in May. Mommy's idea of what a girl needs to take to Europe seems a little off to me. I know that I need more than three pairs of shoes. I feel I need more than three pairs of *evening* shoes. Do you think I'm over-packing? Lucy, Lucy, are you really sad?"

Lucy was always cheerful, forward-thinking, not the least bit *triste*, and there she was lying on the bed with a tear, unmistakably, a tear, rolling down her left cheek.

"But Lucy, you have everything you want. At least, I thought you did. You wanted to marry Tony..."

"Did I? Did I want to marry Tony? I had to." She clapped her hand over her mouth, the moment she said it. She hadn't meant to say it.

95

Mary tried to be delicate. "You don't mean that," said Mary, softly. She brushed the clothes aside and sat down on the bed next to Lucy. "I will remind you. You *were* already engaged. Weren't you?" She had always suspected that Lucy might be further along in her pregnancy than she wanted one to think, but the admission was a little startling. Mary figured Lucy had been two months pregnant when she'd married in December and now that it was May, no amount of clothing could camouflage how far along she was. There had been a litany of excuses. "I was a very big baby. So was Tony." "Mother says I'm eating like a horse." "The Doctor says, the baby may be 11 pounds or more." But Mary had always suspected the other, more logical explanation.

"I shouldn't have told. For the baby's sake, no one should ever know."

"I'll never tell," said Mary.

"Won't you? I believe you won't." She got up and walked across the room and looked out the window onto 52nd Street. A light rain was falling but despite it, life was going on, as usual. "I feel so terribly trapped," she said. "I'll always wonder what else I would have done, who else I might have known, what I would have learned, benefited from, who I would have become." She turned back to Mary and changed her tone. "What color should we paint the nursery? I don't care! There, I've said it. I don't know what I would have done if I'd had the choice."

"You don't mean that. Mother says that pregnancy can make you out of sorts."

"Yes, I guess you could say that," said Lucy, laughing, "that it makes you out of sorts. I have whole places on my thighs I never knew about before, as if they were a three-dimensional road-map. I just wish it hadn't happened so soon. That we'd had more time to just be—free. That I could go to Europe with you. Do I sound spoiled and petulant? You won't tell, will you? Promise me, you'll never tell."

Mary would never tell. But she found it curious

that Lucy had been so judgmental, so eager to expose Lizzie Carswell, and wondered whether it wasn't a version of being harshest on those who possess your own worst faults or perhaps it had been self-protective, that if Lucy was so judgmental, no one would ever suspect her of similar conduct.

"I'm just going to have to learn to live vicariously," said Lucy, sounding much more like herself again. "Show me your shoes. Fashionable boots are always good for Paris. Bring out your evening dresses, one-by-one. Lay them out here on the bed. Promise that you'll send me postcards. No, I'm sorry. I'm afraid I just can't shake this mood. Will you forgive me?" And, with tears streaming down her face, Lucy Collins fled the room. A moment later, Mary heard the sound of the front door closing behind her.

Poor Lucy. It was so strange when someone had seemingly everything they wanted and it turned out to be not what they wanted, at all.

The apartment was empty when Lucy came home. Ivy had left dinner on the stove, a Jamaican lamb stew with vegetables and currants. The rich smell almost brought her to her knees. She had been told the queasiness, the feelings of nausea, would subside by the second part of her pregnancy but, so far, that hadn't occurred. She thought a cup of peppermint tea might soothe her. It was long after seven. Tony wasn't home, yet. She couldn't remember what he'd told her, that he had a meeting, that he was meeting someone for drinks, that he had a dinner. She couldn't remember anything these days and didn't know if that was because she was distracted or if that, too, was a side-effect of her condition.

She had stopped to see the gypsy fortune-teller in the Village. She'd promised Tony that she would not go there anymore but she couldn't help it. It was as if she felt compelled to the little tea shop above the dress shop on 4th Street. There were red geraniums in a vase on the table and a silly crystal ball and, always, a candle burning for effect. The tablecloth was a shade of ivory with a hand-sewn border of gray lace and small round bits of wax had dripped from the burning candle and dried in concentric circles, matching the color of the border. The tea leaves weren't interesting. It was the tarot cards that drew her.

Madame Rosa had a voice that was as deep as a man's and seemed to hold secrets. Her black hair was cut short, sheared, like a cap on her head. Her hands were the one true sign of her age, the fingers, gnarled, with ornate silver rings on all but two of them. Her nails were long and tapered, as if to make a point. There were silver bracelets on her right wrist, one with a large stone that Lucy didn't recognize, deep green, but not with facets, it wasn't an emerald, it wasn't jade, but if you stared at it for a long time, it seemed to change colors as if it had a power of its own.

When she arrived, Madame Rosa had already drawn the blinds and was shutting down for the night. The room smelled faintly of lavender. "Lucia..." That was what Madame Rosa called her. "Lucia, you look so pale. Sit down in this chair, child. No, the easy one." She directed her to a frayed velvet armchair in the corner of the room. She placed a tiny table in front of Lucy and carried over a bentwood chair and placed the deck of cards face down on the table. The back of the cards was emblazoned with a pale pink rose, barely blooming, with a filigreed trellis on either side like a Maxfield Parrish painting. "Lucia..." Madame Rosa seemed to study her. She pushed the deck of cards across the table. "The cards will tell you what to do. Cut the cards. As many times as you want. Make six piles. Good. Now, put them back in any order. The cards know..."

Madame Rosa rested in her chair. She seemed to rock a little, back and forth. "The cards will tell you what to do. But do you want to know?" She picked the deck up. She began to flip the cards over, almost in a sequence on the table. Her bracelets jingled, sounding a bit like bells. Nine cards. Then three more. Rosa looked at the last three and turned them face down, so quickly that Lucy barely caught sight of them. The cards were in French. *L'Ermite*, that was the first one. The Hermit. Of course, she felt alone. *La Lune*, that was the second. The Moon. It made sense that she would draw The Moon, as many believed the moon governed female cycles. The ninth card on the table was *La Justice*. Justice, with its dark meaning, that in the end, you would get what you deserved. Or was that the meaning of the "Judgment" card, a card she hadn't pulled? Lucy couldn't concentrate on Madame Rosa's reading. She heard her say, "I see no light here." She could only think about the three that were face-down on the table, hidden by the painted rose, as if the answer she was seeking lay with them.

She turned them over.

"Are you sure you want to—"

Lucy interrupted. "Yes, I'm sure."

She had already turned the first card over. *La Force*. Strength. On the card, the image of a woman dressed in a long cloak, as if in a fairy tale, with a lion (or was it a fox) trapped between her legs, as she pulled open its powerful jaws.

"You can do anything you set your mind to," said Rosa. "You're very powerful. I've told you this before."

Lucy thought the meaning of the Strength card was ambiguous. How did one get into a position where you needed to tussle with a wolf?

The second was *Le Pendu*. The Hanged Man. A man hanging upside down, wearing the kind of suit a pantomime actor might wear, looking foolish, like a Joker on a playing card, one foot held suspended by a rope, surprised he had been caught in this position. And the third was The Eight of Swords, a woman bound, surrounded by eight swords stuck into the ground, standing upright on a patch of dry sand with water all around, like a makeshift prison island. Nothing ambiguous there. Lucy turned her head away.

Madame Rosa said, almost in a whisper, "Look again, Lucia. The woman's feet are not bound. Only her arms and waist. The water is not so deep. You are holding yourself back. Do not let the fear that led you here, stop you from escaping. The cards know," said Madame Rosa. "The cards will tell you what to do..." But all she saw was a woman bound, surrounded by eight swords, standing on a strip of land surrounded by water.

She left two dollars on the table underneath the tiny vase. This was the second time that she had come this week. She would not buy cut flowers. Tony would not know if she used milk instead of cream. The pin she'd been wanting at the antique store, a little rectangular splash of emerald with a diamond on either side, that she thought would look so pretty on the lapel of her coat, would have to wait. The cards know. The cards knew that she felt trapped and alone. But Madame Rosa thought that she could free herself.

The water she'd put up in the kettle was, finally, boiling. Peppermint tea would soothe her. But what about the other? She pulled out the small paper bag she'd hidden in the back of the spice drawer and opened it. It seemed innocuous enough. An herb with pale green buds lightly flecked with brown.

The smell was strong, unpleasant, myrrh-like, as if a heavy oil coated the leaves. If she were to steep it instead of the peppermint tea. She turned the flame off under the kettle. She needed to think. And then she heard Madame Rosa's voice again. "Look at the card, Lucia. The woman's feet are not bound. She can free herself if she wants to."

When she woke up, she felt lightheaded. The room was white, terribly white, white walls, white sheets that had almost faded to gray, and there was a painting on the wall of yellow daisies in a turquoise vase that she didn't recognize. She hated daisies. The room smelled faintly of iodine. Her head hurt and her legs felt weak, as if they would not support her if she tried to stand. Tony was sitting on the bed. "Luce, we thought we'd lost you."

"I'm not that easy to lose," she said. Her mind was

racing. She remembered that she'd gone to the tea shop on 4th Street. She remembered coming home. She remembered the kettle boiling.

"If Mary hadn't found you, I don't know what would have happened," said Tony.

Mary had found her? She remembered reaching for the counter in the kitchen to steady herself and then nothing more.

"The baby's fine," said Tony. "The doctor said that he can hear the heartbeat. We felt him kick a few minutes ago..." He put his hand lightly on her stomach.

"Him?" said Lucy.

"All right. 'Her'. Whichever one it is. We were worried about *you*. You lost consciousness," said Tony.

"Is that what I did?"

"Yes, you were about to make yourself a cup of tea..."

"And—I fainted like one of those silly girls who

wear their stays too tight?" She was starting to remember, now. The smell of the herbs, alone, had made her feel as if she was about to faint. She remembered reaching for the counter to catch herself.

"The doctor says you're terribly anemic—that you're not getting enough nourishment. I blame myself," said Tony. "I haven't paid enough attention. I've left you alone too much..."

"I should be better at being on my own." She realized how relieved she was that she hadn't lost the baby. They would have a baby. It would look like one of them. It would have her eyes and Tony's confidence. She was having trouble staying awake.

"Lucy, hold my hand. Lucy..."

I washed the teacup," said Mary. "I threw away the herbs." When Lucy next opened her eyes, Mary Nell was standing in the doorway of her hospital room. "You're lucky I'm the one who found you," said Mary. "I came after you. I was worried about you. When you didn't answer the door, I let myself in. I found you lying on the kitchen floor, unconscious. What was it, Lucy? Pennyroyal? Black cohash? You can kill yourself with pennyroyal tea. Did you know that? They talked all about it at one of those suffragette meetings Betsy dragged me to."

"Don't scold me, Mary. I didn't know. I didn't know that it could harm me. I don't know what I was thinking."

"I was terrified," said Mary. "I didn't know if they would come in time. I ran down to the doorman and he called for an ambulance and I didn't know if you would be all right." Mary walked across the room and sat down on Lucy's bed. "I washed your cheek where you'd cut yourself when you'd fallen. I saw the teacup and the herbs and I washed them before they came. I didn't know if you were going to be all right."

"I'm frightened, too. That's why I did it. Please, forgive me," she said. "I feel so weak," she said. "I don't know if I'll be any good at this. I'm good at—looking pretty. If a man speaks to me, I always come back with something quick. How is one quick with a baby? I was so frightened. I felt so alone."

"Don't cry, Lucy. It can't be good for you. The doctor says you need to rest."

"Did the doctor know?"

"No. He didn't guess. He thinks you're anemic. I didn't tell him what you did. I won't tell anyone. I can keep a secret."

"Can any of us keep a secret, Mary?"

It was, then, that there was a knock at the door. It was Tony. "May I come in?"

"Yes," said Mary, "she's almost decent."

Yes, Mama, of course, I'll use good judgment..." "No, Papa, I promise, I'll be careful..." In her mind, she was running off a check-list of her packing. *Two pairs, sensible shoes.* She worried that she hadn't brought enough clothes for evening or that the ones she had brought would be out-dated. She worried that she might feel out of place in Europe, like one of those tourists in New York in pastel clothes. "Yes, Papa, I will be careful of strangers, I promise, even if they're properly introduced. Yes, I am making fun of you a bit, Papa." She strained to get a glimpse of Betsy Owen or Geoffrey Rice but saw no trace of either of them. Her parents had discovered a few days before that Geoffrey was traveling with them and, curiously, were overjoyed. Mary's mother had said, "I'm so relieved. I was worried about—I know you'll think I'm old-fashioned—but I was worried about three women traveling alone." Mary stood on her tiptoes to try to spot Iris Ogleby in the crowd but couldn't find her either. She worried Iris might have missed the boat. "No, Papa, I promise, I'll be careful."

"Just kiss her, John, and let her go."

Her bags were given to a steward. "I love you both," she said. And, then, she made her way up the gangplank, looking, for all the world, like a young girl who had everything she wanted.

꧁꧂

There was excitement in the air and the heavy smell of French perfume, as the boat prepared to leave New York Harbor, men in waistcoats on the deck, as the morning was quite chilly, little girls in patent leather boots holding on to their mothers' hands, all clinging to the rail for a last sight of shore.

There was a woman standing on the deck who fascinated Mary. She was wearing a blue silk dress with a drop waist and a double skirt, the slightly plunging neckline edged with a thin line of gray fox. She was ultra-thin, without a line in her face, her bobbed hair just peeking out from a cloche hat that was ringed with the same fur as her neckline. Mary recognized her from the society pages. Elizabeth Nash. She'd graduated from Vassar. Just 22, she was an editor of one of those women's magazines. And anything she chose to do became the fashion overnight. Mary wondered what it would be like to be so confident, so at ease with being on display.

She looked around for Betsy Owen or Geoffrey Rice, even Iris Ogleby would do, but saw no sign of any of them. Above her, on the forward deck, the ship's orchestra began a subdued version of *La Marseillaise* which became more spirited as some of the crowd began to sing. There were no champagne corks popping. Not until they reached the 12-mile limit. Mary saw her parents on the dock waving, her mother in an unfashionable brown broad-brimmed hat that she insisted was utilitarian and quite kept the sun off her face. Her mother said if something was utilitarian, it did not need to be fashionable. For an odd, fleeting moment, Mary wondered if she would ever return to New York. She realized she was being dramatic and she would, of course. But then she thought about Lizzie Carswell and wondered whether Lizzie would ever return. Had her father really sent her to be a nanny in Switzerland? What happened to girls who worked as *au pairs*? She wondered whether Lizzie Carswell's father had even waited on the dock long enough to wave good-bye.

And then she felt a hand on her back. She looked up and saw Geoffrey Rice. He looked so calm. "I'm glad I found you," he said. "Did you settle in?"

"No, not the least bit. We were—I was late."

"I settled Betsy in," said Geoffrey. "She needs more looking after than you would think."

The ship listed to one side as it prepared to pull away from the harbor. Mary held onto the railing and turned to face the shore, so that her parents could get a last sight of her, if they were looking. She waved, although the faces of the people on the dock were, now, almost indistinguishable from one another. "The last time I did this," said Geoffrey, "I was on a military ship. There were thousands of people on the dock, it seemed like thousands, waving flags. We were so young and so enthusiastic." He sounded bitter. Behind them, the skyline of New York appeared etched in black, almost like a still photograph.

"Would you enlist again?" asked Mary.

"Knowing what I know now, if the circumstances were the same? Yes, probably. Third generation military and all that. I would feel obliged. But there was, also, a sense that we were needed, that we were appreciated in the French countryside. That wasn't the part that went wrong. It wasn't like the Philippines, where we went to, essentially, take over. There was a sense in France that we had come to liberate them. But none of us were prepared for the reality of war." He caught himself. "I didn't mean to go off on that."

Above them on the forward deck, the orchestra began to play a melody that sounded like a Germanic waltz with vibrant, swelling stringed instruments as the ship again swayed to one side and began to pull forcefully away from the shore.

The boat was called *The Paris,* a French luxury steamship that sailed across the Atlantic for much of 1926 from Le Havre to New York and back again, like a commuter train, with its precious cargo of travelers and immigrants. The first class section was richly furnished with silk couches, crystal chandeliers and Aubusson carpets. The Grand Salon had a beveled glass ceiling that was cut in sections like a dome and an enormous fireplace with a carved mantel that burned, from six a.m. to midnight, cherry wood and pine. There was a

Salon de Conversation, which was smaller and more intimate than the Grand Salon, with an honor bar that was open night and day, a gymnasium with a weight-reduction machine that resembled a large rubber band that fit around one's rear, barbells, a squash court, an enormous tiled swimming pool and a bevy of masseuses at one's beck and call, a library with books in seven languages, a formal ballroom with a twelve-piece orchestra and dancing every night, a French chef and an Italian chef, and an acting troupe on board. Mary took to calling the ship "*The Paree*", her homage to Billy Holmes' gay and antic grandmother.

Billy and Clara had sailed the week before on a ship very much like theirs, *The France*, and then taken a train to Rome. They were due to meet up with them in Paris in June. At least, that was the present plan.

Mary shared a first-class cabin, a suite, with Iris Ogleby, her parents' way of off-setting the cost of her travel. It was a charming suite, with a bedroom and a sitting room that was over-done, a chintz sofa, and paisley pillows that were mismatched but complementary. Iris was understanding of the fact that she was an add-on and let Mary have the bed with the view out the porthole and the top two drawers of the dresser. Mary learned, even though it was useless information, that Iris curled her hair at night in paper wrappers and had a better figure than one would imagine, with a tiny waist and shapely legs and, actually, a pretty cleavage. She would suggest to Iris when they got to Paris that Iris cut her hair, shear to the chin, like Louise Brooks in *The American Venus*.

The first night, Betsy Owen was invited to sit at the captain's table, which she did, with Geoffrey Rice, and then opted for her own table with her traveling companions as her party for the duration of the crossing.

"It's too much like performing," said Betsy Owen. "They expect me to be clever. They think it's amusing when I'm acerbic. If I publish again, I will 'perform' again. I didn't take this trip to entertain anyone but myself and perhaps you, dear," she said to Mary.

Mary wondered what it would be like to be invited to sit at the captain's table, to have people think you were amusing and acerbic, to be a draw, to be a published and recognized author. Mary was working on a piece, now, that seemed to be taking on a life of its own. She'd always written verse before, but this was more like a novel or a novella. It was a touch autobiographical, veiled but recognizable, someone *had* told her once that it was best to write about what you know. She was looking forward to working on her book in Paris. Everyone always talked about how brilliant the light was in Paris, diffused and radiant, at the same time, and said that the city, itself, was inspirational. She had wired ahead to the hotel to request that a writing desk be placed in her room. In Paris, she would have a room of her own.

Her parents had wanted her to share a room at the hotel with Iris Ogleby, but she had pleaded. "No, Papa," she'd said. "You know how I get when I don't have time on my own. It makes me awfully nervous. I don't want to be nervous in Paris. It will be hard enough being away from you and Mama."

Her father admitted that she had always needed to have time on her own. "It's our fault," her father said, finally. "I guess it comes of being an only child." And then he teased her, "I wonder what will happen to you when you're married."

"That's different, Papa, and you know it. Husbands respect you when you're moody." And she threw her arms around his neck and kissed him because she knew that he'd relented.

On the ship, Geoffrey's behavior towards Mary was flattering, at first. He was attentive and amusing, but the intimacy they'd had, the possibility of the intimacy they could have, had been eroded by their day-to-day camaraderie. Perhaps it was because of their close proximity to one another, that ship-life required that one have breakfast, lunch, and dinner with one's traveling companions, she worried he was beginning to take her for granted and treat her the way one would a sibling or a friend. She began to be nervous when she was around him. She contrived to spend more time alone with Iris. She fretted over the deficiencies in her wardrobe, the imagined puffiness under her eyes. It took all of a day and a half for her to turn into the type of woman she'd never had much patience for. It was so difficult to look pretty all of the time.

On the third day of the voyage, the seas turned rough, requiring them to stay in their cabins lying down. The ocean was so wild, the boat felt like a toy being tossed in the water. The Captain said the storm would last for three hours but after six hours, it seemed as if it would never end.

It came up all of a sudden. Mary was lying on a lounge chair on the deck with Iris Ogleby, reading *The Great Gatsby* and taking in the sun. She was just at the part where Jordan was explaining to Nick that

Gatsby had bought the house so that Daisy would be just across the bay, when the air seemed to change. First, it was the wind. It was just a bit of wind but it caught their attention. A copy of *Metropolitan Life* flew off a table next to them and skittered across the deck. The skies turned dark in the distance. As it began to rain, they ran inside to the Grand Salon for cover. There were six-foot swells. The Captain came in and made a brief speech, that it was a storm, that it shouldn't last more than three hours, that he thought they would be more comfortable if they went to their cabins and lay down. He apologized for its brevity as his presence was required on the starboard deck, in the navigation room, anywhere that might be useful. The Captain had a scattered air about him in the best of times.

The stewards escorted them to their cabins and, every thirty minutes or so, knocked on the cabin doors to see if an assistance was required. Iris was so pale, nauseous, and bordering on delusional, that on the second room-check, it was determined she might be better off in the infirmary. Mary wanted to accompany her but Frederick, the fresh-faced steward who had been assigned to them, insisted it might be safer if Mary stayed in the cabin. She didn't mind the solitude. She thought she might have slept a bit but the sound of the rain and the raging ocean waters was so intrusive that she wasn't sure. She was ill two or three times more. After the last, she half crawled back to the bed and lay down. She was lying on her back, trying to find a pattern in the ceiling that might be soothing, almost as if it was a meditation exercise—Lucy had once taught her to breathe like a yogi.

It took her a moment to realize the rain had ended, that the boat was rocking gently, the way it had before the storm began. She stood and it took her a moment to get her balance. She was thirsty. She'd been so ill, it occurred to her she might be dehydrated. She made her way up the stairs to the first-class deck. The sea was eerily still and in the distance there were clouds and evidence of swells. It wasn't as if it had stopped, it was as if they'd sailed away from the storm, into a kinder weather system.

The first-class deck was deserted, at least, that's what she thought, at first. And then she heard laughter at the other end of the deck, muffled laughter, as if someone had a secret. It was Elizabeth Nash, the editor of that women's magazine and the young woman she was traveling with, who Mary thought might be her assistant. Elizabeth Nash was wearing slacks and a simple, stylish cashmere jacket, looking a bit like an ad for an afternoon on a first class deck. Mary saw her lean in to her companion. It took her a moment to realize they were kissing. She stood and watched them, feeling a bit like a voyeur, and, at the same time, as if she was watching something in a photograph, unable to tear her eyes away from them, at first. She wondered what it would be like to be so free. She caught herself and turned away and walked quickly into the Grand Salon.

The stewards were still cleaning up. A large upholstered chair had overturned. Some books had fallen from the shelf on the other side of the fireplace. A few prisms had fallen from the chandelier and shattered on the floor.

Mary had just sat down on a small sofa in front of a table and ordered herself a cup of tea when Iris appeared in the Grand Salon.

"I've met the most wonderful man in the infirmary," Iris announced.

"How is that possible?" asked Mary.

"He's an art dealer," said Iris, as if that explained everything.

"Was he ill?"

"No, he's traveling with a painter who was ill. Claude Bresson."

"The art dealer?"

"No, the painter."

"I'm a little confused," said Mary.

"I'm a little confused, too," said Iris. "I didn't think that it was possible."

Mary resisted the impulse to laugh at her. "Start at the beginning," she said. "I'll order you some tea. Do you think you could drink tea?"

"Yes, please. And do you think they might have some toast, too?"

Iris sat down across from Mary, settling herself in a comfortable arm chair. Whether it was the effect of the illness or not, she looked almost pretty, her cheeks flushed, as if she was excited. Her hair brushed back from her face, unintentionally, so that the line of her eyebrow was visible. Mary had never noticed before, Iris had the kind of eyebrows models covet, thick, perfectly lined, almost as if they had been filled in with the thinnest kohl, so that her blue eyes and pale eyelashes seemed accentuated by them. "I feel as if I might have a sip of brandy, too," said Iris, "but that might be pushing it, don't you think?"

"Yes, I do," said Mary. "Start with the toast. Perhaps I'll have some, too."

"Have you ever felt," asked Iris, "as if you were looking at someone under glass?" She sounded a little breathless. "That's what I felt like. I was feeling so ill and I tried to sit up and I felt a man's hand on my back and I looked up and there he was. I knew at once he wasn't a steward or a doctor. 'Are you all right, dear?' he said. I almost swooned. Not because his hand was on my back but because I felt so ill. And he caught me. In his arms. And when I opened my eyes, it was like I was looking at him from far-away and up close at the same time, the way something looks when it's under glass. He has the kindest face. I must have looked puzzled as if I wondered why he was at my bedside because he explained to me that his friend was ill. His name is Maurice. Maurice Chabon." She said this last as if she was pronouncing the name of a hat. "Don't you think that's a lovely name? He stayed with me, at my bedside. He found a wet cloth which he held on my forehead. It was cool and reassuring and awfully calming. The Doctor was busy with Maurice's friend and an older woman, Mrs. Olive Pendergast, who was having such a hard time they, finally, gave her a shot to settle her down. The doctor wanted to give me a shot, as well, but I was frightened that I might be asleep if there was something that I needed to be awake for. I mean, if the storm got worse or something. The doctor said the best thing I could do was rest, I was feeling so weak, and Maurice said he'd stay with me, so I relented. It was lovely. I think it was like twilight sleep. Have you ever heard women talk about that, who've been through childbirth? A kind of ecstasy of feeling nothing.

"When I woke up, he was still there. It was as if no time had passed. It is a lovely drug, whatever it is they give you. I think I still feel the effects of it, now.

Or else, it's the effects of something else. He already has a pet name for me, 'Buttercup'. It sounds so funny when he says it with his accent, 'But-ter-cup'. Do you think you can fall in love that quickly?"

"Now, Iris, slow down a little bit. Drink your tea. No, drink your tea slowly. I'm sure you don't know hardly anything about him."

"But don't you think," said Iris, "you can some-times know, just on one encounter, a person's true character?"

"Well, perhaps. But maybe you should see how you feel in a few days and how he behaves towards you."

"All right," said Iris. "That makes sense. But I bet it will be lovely."

By the time they had their tea and returned to the cabin, Maurice Chabon had arranged for a dozen long stem white roses, dramatically displayed in a tall black fan-shaped vase, to be delivered to the room, with a note.

> *Buttercup,*
> *I hope you're feeling better.*
> > *affectionately,*
> > *Maurice*

"So far, I'd say, he's behaving well," said Iris, sounding like a contented cat. Not that Mary was jealous but she was surprised to find that, when it came right down to it, she was a more cautious person than Iris.

Frederick, their attentive steward, knocked on their door an hour later, bearing a small silver tray with a note on it. "Miss Ogleby," he said, quite formally, "if it is all right with you, I will wait. The gentleman has requested a reply."

> *Dear Buttercup,*
> *If you are feeling better, would you meet for a*
> *late supper in the Petit Salon at 9:00?*
> > *your faithful servant,*
> > *Maurice*

"Your faithful servant?" said Mary, rolling her eyes.

"I think that shows he has a sense of humor," said Iris. And she reached for the pen to reply.

"No, wait," said Mary. "You're not thinking about going, are you? I think you should not appear to be so easy. Frederick, you're not hearing any of this. Perhaps you should write, 'Better but not quite. Perhaps another time.'"

"Don't you think that's a little cold? I mean, that's not how I feel, at all. Couldn't I—go?"

"It would not be advisable to appear to be too anxious," said Mary. "If he's so enamored of you, he'll wait."

"And if he doesn't?" Iris asked sheepishly.

"Better to know that, now," said Mary. "And, Frederick, will you make it seem as if it's true? Could you tell him, we've ordered broth to the room. And could we? Order broth for Miss Ogleby and, I guess, the same for me. Beef broth. Chicken always make you feel as if you're ill. And a little toast? Could you eat more toast, Iris? I could. I could eat a plate of toast."

"Yes, Miss Nell," said Frederick, trying to suppress a smile.

"All right, then," said Iris, not looking the least bit happy about the decision. "Couldn't I write, sort of what you said, 'My Dear Maurice...'"

"Do you have to call him that?"

"Yes, I do. Thank you. I am feeling better but not altogether. *Might* we do it another time? Anyway, no matter what you say, that is what I'll write," said Iris, putting her foot down in a modest way. She pulled a sheet of notepaper and scribbled on it and sealed it in an envelope and wrote on the front of the envelope, Maurice Chabon, with a little bit of a flourish underneath the *M* and the *C* and the *n* in his name.

"And, we'll see," said Mary. "We'll see what he does."

"Whatever he does," said Iris, "I bet it will be lovely."

B ut *do* we really know anything about him?" asked Mary.

"He has a gallery in Paris," said Betsy Owen, "which might mean he has a fair amount of money, even if some of it *is* in art. On the other hand," she sighed, "he could be a—an operator, what do you call them...?"

"A hustler," said Mary.

"Some of them are. But," said Betsy, "he seems solid and down to earth, if a little slick..."

"Suspiciously charming," said Mary. "I'll say he's attentive. He hasn't let her out of his sight for the last two days. I sort of miss her. Don't tell her I said that. And he's middle-aged and rather funny looking, don't you think?"

"He is a bit older than Iris," said Betsy, "that's true. But you didn't expect she would attract a matinee idol, did you? Or what is it you call them, a sheik? Or someone like Geoffrey?"

Mary tried to stop herself from blushing.

"You shouldn't talk about me like that, Aunt Betsy," said Geoffrey, "when I'm in the room."

Betsy smiled. "But that's what's nice about Maurice," she said. "He doesn't seem complicated, at all. I know you'd be bored in a minute, Mary, but...he's forthright and honest and he follows her around like a lost puppy."

"Forthright? Honest? I don't trust him. Did you see the necklace he gave her? Why would a man travel on a boat with a yellow amethyst necklace? On the off chance he met a woman he wanted to give it to?"

"Do you think there's a lesson there, Mary? Beware of men who travel with necklaces?"

"Geoffrey, tell her," said Mary. "Did you come on this boat with jewelry?"

"No, none that I can think of," said Geoffrey.

"I'm sure there's a perfectly reasonable explanation as to why he had a necklace, perhaps he bought it at an estate sale along with some paintings," said Betsy, pleased with herself for coming up with something slightly plausible so quickly.

"He said he thought it would look pretty on her. Don't make fun of me for being cautious," said Mary. "Have you seen it? It's quite a statement. I was a little surprised that she accepted it. I can't help it. Something about him makes me nervous. And every time I voice it, all she says is," mimicking Iris when she said it, "'I'm sure whatever he does, it will be lovely.'"

M ary, wake up." She heard Iris call her almost as if it was in a dream. The steamship whistle was sounding loudly. "We're almost there."

It was just after dawn when *The Paris* began the last leg of its journey, into the dock at Le Havre. Mary and Iris pulled their clothes on and went up to the deck to catch the first sight of land. The water was turquoise, the harbor fogged in a bit and the light from the rising sun was soft, diffuse, and it seemed as if they were entering into an impressionist painting as the boat began to pull into the harbor. Mary felt her mood shift from one of excitement to one of almost quiet bliss.

The band was playing *La Marseillaise*, softly, on the deck above them. The people waiting on the dock appeared like specks of gray, as if they, too, had been painted in watercolor.

As if echoing Mary's thoughts, Maurice was describing to Iris the things they would do in Paris. "Of course, the Eiffel Tower, Buttercup, but to sit on one of the bridges of the Seine when the light is like this is almost like being in a painting. The Eiffel Tower makes you understand Braque. But the Seine makes you understand Monet."

Mary looked at the sailing boats resting in the harbor. They would take a train and tonight they would sleep in Paris.

She heard Maurice say to Iris, "To be in love in Paris, Buttercup—"

Mary interrupted him, "But to be in love any-where else in the world, that is the true test."

"You are a cynic," said Maurice, laughing.

"Am I?" said Mary. "I never thought of myself that way." In truth, Mary wasn't cynical about her own life but she was cynical about Iris's and she was certain that Iris was, presently, having a summer fling that was destined to end badly.

"She's not a cynic. She's a realist," said Geoffrey Rice, who'd come up behind Mary and put his arms around her waist. "She can even be romantic if the situation calls for it."

"But," said Mary, "only after careful considera-tion." She thought she felt Geoffrey brush the top of her hair with his lips. The harbor was clouded in a pale bluish mist and she realized she didn't have to try to be romantic if this was what her life was like.

The train ride from Le Havre to St. Lazare Station took five and a half hours. Out the window, the lush, green meadows of Normandy were visible, a slight bend and the first fingers of the Seine, blue and docile at its start, the 17th century town of Rouen, with steep, narrow cobblestoned streets, through a round stone tunnel that seemed almost magical to Mary, and then a straightshot through the industrial outskirts of Paris.

A French family, two grandparents, a young mother, and an adorable 4-year-old named Thérèse with a mop of curly hair sat across from them in the crowded train compartment. The grandmother, Hélène, insisted that they share a picnic dinner, heavily crusted bread, a coarse pâté, tiny pickles that were a little sour, a roasted chicken, and a round of brie that had melted so that it was almost the consistency of butter and made the train car smell a bit. It was determined that Geoffrey had been stationed, for a time, in Lyons not far from the family's home and they revealed that their oldest son, Jean-Pierre, had been killed in one of the early skirmishes in the Meuse-Argonne Offensive. Hélène had no bitterness, only pride, about her son's actions and wore his medal on her lapel which she showed to them proudly, a cross with a blue ribbon.

Thérèse, the little girl, sat on Mary's lap after dinner and Mary helped her draw a bunny rabbit and a cat in charcoal on a large piece of white paper. Mary learned the name for rabbit, *"le lapin"*, and cat, *"le chat"*. The little girl explained to Mary that the

bunny rabbit and the cat were friends, "*les amis*".
Geoffrey was sleeping in the window seat with his
head almost resting on Mary's shoulder. The little
girl asked Mary if Mary and Geoffrey were friends.
"Les amis?"

"Yes," Mary answered softly, "I suppose you could
say that. But I would hope that we were more than
friends." Thérèse, of course, didn't understand
Mary's reply, as Mary had answered in English. She
asked again. "Les amis?"

"Oui," said Mary, "I guess that would be one way
to describe us."

Before the family disembarked at Rouen, in a
rush of overcoats, umbrellas, and wicker suitcases,
there was a great exchange of addresses and a promise exacted, good for the next twenty years (that
would, most likely, never be kept), to visit them in
Lyons. Thérèse left Mary the picture of the bunny
rabbit and the cat. At the bottom she had written, in
block childlike letters, LES AMIS.

Their first few days in Paris were spent, as Betsy Owen called it, acclimatizing. Betsy thought, she actually had a theory about it, that the best way to get to know a city was to immerse yourself in it, to pretend that you lived there and forego, at least, at first, traditional sightseeing.

On the third day, Mary Nell went on her own to Notre Dame, early in the morning, almost as if it was a vigil. There were prisms of light coming in through the stained glass rose windows. She had read about the rose windows, a tribute to Mary and the Apostles, but no picture could do justice to the sheer majesty and the pink and crimson shafts of light that shone through.

There was a young woman at the front of the cathedral who Mary thought looked familiar, wearing a scarf tied over her head, kneeling, and saying a prayer. Mary's attention was drawn back to the shafts of light coming in through the rose window—as if one really was in the presence of God—and the images of the stained glass itself. She couldn't imagine the artistry that had gone into the pictures depicting the Apostles. And when she looked back to the front pew, the young woman was gone. She looked around the cathedral but saw no sign of her.

She thought about taking the steps up to the bell tower, Victor Hugo and all that, but already a line had formed at the stairs. She lit a candle and said a prayer. She put a few coins in the collection box, made slight use of the holy water, and took a taxi back to the hotel.

No. 12 Rue du Dragon, that was the address she had given him on the small slip of paper. It wasn't entirely a residential neighborhood. There were houses and apartment buildings interspersed with shops and a small hotel on the corner that looked as if it might have, at one time, been a large private home. It was a respectable neighborhood, in a comfortable, shabby old-friend kind of way. The building itself was stone, in need of a coat of paint, but with elaborate molding as if its initial construction had been artfully conceived.

Geoffrey Rice hesitated, then rang the concierge bell. After a moment, an old woman, all dressed in gray, a gray kerchief covering her gray hair, opened the door for him and let him into the courtyard. It was as if he had taken a step back in time or into the garden of an Italian villa perched on a hill. There was a stone fountain affixed to the wall, a splash of water flowing into its bowl from the mouth of a carved stone dragon. There were large stone urns brimming with white azaleas, and lilac, and sprays of small pink roses.

He wondered if the tiny bird-like woman who opened the door was the concierge. He tried to speak to her in French but she did not respond, seeming to look past him. He handed her the small slip of paper and she gestured to a stone staircase at the back of the courtyard. He took the stone steps up to *No. 5* and used the knocker carved in the shape of a dragon's head.

Lizzie Carswell gave a small laugh when she saw

him. "It is so nice to see a familiar face," she said. "I've been shut in for days."

She was much prettier, even, than he'd remembered. Her long dark hair framed her face, her skin was the color of alabaster and unflawed. She was rail-thin but with a certain strength and attitude that came from confidence and, clearly, a love of mischief.

"I told you I'd look in on you."

"Yes, people say that often and don't mean it."

She walked across the living room and pulled back the blue silk curtains letting the light in through the windows. "How are you?" she said. "Is it strange for you to be back in France in such— different times?"

He realized she was the first person who'd asked him that. It was such a simple, direct question, but had everything to do with what he'd been feeling about being back in Europe in peace-time.

"I'm having trouble getting used to it," he said.

"I keep feeling as if any moment I'm going to be called up or, as if it's all play-acting and, any moment, someone will lift up the curtain and underneath it, there will still be a war. Does that seem strange to you?"

"No, not really."

"I've thought about going back to Montfaucon," he said, "my own private vigil, as if it would give me peace but I'm afraid it might have the opposite effect, as if I might find something there that would haunt me forever. I don't mean to be so dark. As if I have nightmares when I'm awake."

"How could you be otherwise?"

"No, I'm sorry. And I've come to see how you are getting along."

"Me? I'm well. Quite well, considering. Better than you, it seems. Follow me, into the kitchen," she said, reminding him of a butterfly as she flitted about the apartment, "I'm afraid I've become quite domestic."

There was a chicken slowly cooking in a red clay pot on the stove and he watched as she chopped a bit of dill and tossed it in, and a half a cup of wine, laughing as she poured it in. "I've already prepared tonight's dinner," she said. "It's funny how competent you can be when you're the one in charge." She turned the flame off under the chicken. "There, it will be fine."

"Can I take you out?" asked Geoffrey, on a whim. "It's such a lovely afternoon."

"When? Now?"

"Yes, why not. Is anybody here?"

"No. I don't have an obligation for hours."

"We could have lunch and walk along the Champs Élysées. I haven't been there."

"I'm not sure I—should leave. I might be needed here. It's funny to feel *so* responsible."

"It will do you good, I think. Just for a few hours."

"All right. If you promise it will just be for a few hours." It was only a moment before she got a sweater and brushed her hair.

He realized she wasn't like any of the well-heeled

women that he'd known, all cut from the same cloth, opinionated, well-protected, predictable, even when they pushed at the edges of convention. Lizzie seemed so competent on her own and yet he knew she must be fragile. It was admirable that she'd made the best of the hand that had been dealt her, seemingly without complaining. No, it was more than that, it was the sound of her laugh and that she could laugh, at the simplest things, the oddness that he'd come to see her or the simple act of pouring wine into a pot-au-feu. And she was so pretty, without artifice or affect. She was wearing the plainest clothes, a brown skirt, a white blouse, and sensible shoes, and yet he thought she was the loveliest, yes, perhaps, the most beautiful woman he'd ever seen.

"Promise you won't tell the others that you've seen me," she said. "I felt—I don't feel any of them wish me well. And the last thing I want is their sympathy. I'm surprised that I gave you the address..."

She had given him the address when he'd

stopped by to see her the morning that he'd gone to look for Billy Holmes. Betsy Owen had suggested that he stop by and see Lizzie. She hadn't been particularly helpful. She was protective of Billy and vague about what had occurred the night before, implying that it was somehow Billy's story to tell. Not that any of it mattered to her, as she was leaving. She was in a bit of a rush, packing, she was leaving for Europe the next day. And when he told her that he thought he might be in Paris, she'd written the address down on a piece of paper and said that if he was in Paris, this was where he might find her. He'd promised he'd look in on her.

"Promise," she repeated, "you won't tell them that you've seen me."

"I'll promise. But only if you'll promise that you'll see me again."

She laughed at that, and he found himself all afternoon trying to say or do things that would effect a laugh again.

June 2, 1926

Dear Lucy,

Congratulations on the birth of Rose! Mother sent a wire and says she's very beautiful. I'm sure I'll see her when I return in a month and that she'll already be doing clever things like charming everyone in the room. Returning, though, is not the first thing on my mind. I have tried to squeeze everything I can from this experience, hardly wanting to sleep, at all. Have you ever seen Monet's painting of the Seine? I think that is my aspiration, no, not to paint, but to see things in the way that he did, where the light is diffuse and yet clear. Or to write the way Millay does, where everything becomes a metaphor but on the surface is quite clear. Did you know that she insisted on being called Vincent in high school? I wish that I could be as free a creature as she is. But I have always felt bound by convention.

We went to a little hotel called The Benedict for tea on Tuesday. And at the table next to us was the writer Ernest Hemingway, whose new novel about the '20's and Paris is, supposedly, going to be all the rage. He was a little drunk, even though it was the afternoon, as were the people with him. I don't think he likes Betsy very much. Although he did condescend to say to her, "You would have made a very good journalist." None of us quite knew what that meant. Although, I believe, he holds journalism in high regard, it might have been an indictment of her *fiction. I felt as if I should hang on his every word but, honestly, it was disappointing as he was so messy and so attuned to the adoration of those around him. As if it was all a big circle he needed to draw around himself.*

Geoffrey is attentive, although not entirely the way I want him to be. He is terribly protective of me and, I think, he is one of the things he wants to protect me from. Something dark happened to him. Do you think it happens to all soldiers who see battle? He won't really talk about it. I think he might have night terrors. Is that what they call them? He knocked on my door the other night at 4 a.m. and made me go out with him for a walk. It was lovely, peaceful and exciting at the same time. To be the only people on the Pont Neuf except for a constable who smiled at us, as if we were lovers.

I have to go. I'll write again later.

Lots of love, to all of you,
Mary

∞

Mary had been asleep. They had been at the Ritz earlier that night at the bar drinking pink ladies. The bartender had given her a lesson in mixing them, a shot of gin, calvados, an egg-white, the rim of the glass dipped in the finest granulated sugar. After the fourth round, she was almost proficient and everyone in the room except an Arab man who drank only champagne had sampled them. Someone was playing the piano, a sort of light ragtime tune reminiscent of home and, then, a softer melody. They'd danced a bit. Geoffrey had held her, so lightly, all she had been aware of was his fingertips on the small of her back and that her feet seemed to follow his almost without meaning to. And, then, the music ended and the lights came on in the bar. Not yet wanting the night to end, they'd stopped at a café on the way back to the hotel. Geoffrey had ordered calvados and coffee. She had ordered only calvados and smoked a bit of a French cigarette,

159

enough to start a headache and decide that Turkish tobacco would not be a taste she would acquire. Surely, it couldn't be morning already. Someone was knocking on the door. Her head hurt. She wondered if she had any aspirin. Lucy had told her once that it was best to take aspirin before you woke up with a headache. She wondered if she had missed that moment.

There was a knock again and then she heard him through the door, "It's Geoffrey, will you let me in?"

She worried about the propriety of letting him into her room in the middle of the night and then wished it hadn't occurred to her to worry. She put on the silk kimono Lucy had given her for her last birthday. There wasn't anything to do about her hair.

She opened the door. "I couldn't sleep," he said. "I hope you don't mind. I sometimes think sleep is overrated. I thought you might—come and take a walk with me." He settled himself in the easy chair in the corner of the room as if it was perfectly natural that he would be in her room in the middle of the night. "I thought we could see what the city looks like in what my mother calls pale morning."

His hair was tousled and he looked young and strong, and yet, there was something old about his eyes, as if he knew things that other people could only imagine. Of course, she didn't mind that he'd awakened her. She sent him down to the lobby to wait for her while she changed.

The city was still and quiet. They walked toward the Seine. There wasn't anyone on the street except a few fruit vendors setting up their stalls at an open market.

The morning was gray in the hour before the sun begins to rise. The bridge itself reflected on the river. There was a barge sailing so smoothly it barely seemed to ripple the water as it passed beneath them. The morning air was chilly. It almost seemed as if time had stopped.

"Did you have a nightmare?" asked Mary.

"Something like one," he said. "It's not the dream so much as the way I feel when I wake up. As if the world has changed and there's no escaping. I can't fall back to sleep. The only thing that helps is walking."

"Mother thinks, if one tells a dream, it doesn't come true."

"It's more like a memory, though, told in a dream." He didn't say anything more.

She imagined it was about the war. And perhaps he was right to spare her the details although she did think if one just confronted one's fears, it was better.

"Do you have them?" he asked her.

"Nightmares? Not really. Sometimes I worry that terrible things will happen—but I do that when I'm awake."

"What kind of things?"

"You'll laugh. I don't know how to say it so you won't. I worry that things won't turn out the way I want them to. See, I told you that you'd laugh at me.

It's getting light. The color of the river's changing. It's turning blue. See, the robin there. It's calling someone. Stop it, Geoffrey. I'm trying to change the subject. You promised that you wouldn't laugh at me."

They had walked out almost to the middle of the Pont Neuf, which many believe is the most beautiful bridge in Paris. The sun was starting to rise over the trees. They heard voices, a little boy calling, "Maman!" and the sound of a car engine starting, as if the city had started to awake. They were still alone on the bridge. They saw the shape of a man walking towards them, a constable, who smiled at them as if they were lovers and continued on.

As they walked back to the hotel, the outdoor fruit market was open. Geoffrey stepped into a patisserie to buy them each a coffee and a croissant. Mary noticed the shape of a young woman at a fruitstand, buying a basket of apricots. Her hair was tied back in a scarf and her face was barely visible, but there was something familiar about the way she stood, holding her weight on her right leg, slightly, fashionably slouched. It occurred to her that the young woman might be Lizzie Carswell. She started to follow her but the young woman rushed on through the crowd and disappeared into the court-yard of a building.

They were three women on an afternoon's excursion, Betsy Owen, Iris Ogleby, and Mary Nell. Geoffrey Rice had begged off, saying he had something else to do. Who could blame him? Mary assumed he was tired of the society of women. She had not so much tolerance for it herself. She had a moment where she wondered where he was but then her attention was drawn to the exquisite scenery and the expanse of lake that surrounded them.

"It is rather like something a tourist would do.

I recognize that," said Betsy Owen as they were on a ferry on their way to one of the long thin islands of the Bois de Boulogne. "But sometimes those are the best things to do."

"I thought we were supposed to 'acclimatize'," said Mary, teasing her.

"We have acclimatized and, now, we're allowed to be tourists," said Betsy. She was wearing all white, a long flowing white skirt that camouflaged her round figure, a white blouse, a white hat, and a white shawl with the tiniest amount of purple, some sort of flower, in its pattern, as if she had dressed appropriately for a garden party. "I went here once when I was first married," she went on. "It was lovely."

"Please, don't ever say that again," said Iris.

"Say what?" said Betsy.

"She didn't mean anything by it," said Mary.

"What do you mean I didn't mean anything by it?" asked Betsy.

"No, not you. Iris."

"I did. I absolutely meant it," said Iris. "Please don't ever say that again."

"All right," said Betsy. "I won't."

Betsy wondered whether they'd reached that part of the vacation where they'd spent too much time with one another or if something else was at play. She had thought it odd that Iris hadn't come down for breakfast. Iris always came down for breakfast. Mary reported that when she went to find her in her room, it was after eleven, Iris hadn't dressed yet and her eyes were puffy, as if she had been crying. Iris brushed it off and insisted she'd had too much wine the night before and had difficulty sleeping. But that wasn't it.

She had gone to dinner with Maurice at a restaurant in the Champs Élysées that looked like an elegant summer cottage with tiny panes of glass, like a greenhouse, and a view outside of the imposing chestnut trees, an old-style, formal establishment that was as comfortable as it was stylish.

They had barely sat down and ordered a bottle of wine when Maurice said, "Buttercup, I have something to tell you." They were sitting at a table in the window at Ledoyen, having been to an exhibit at the Grand Palais. Maurice nodded to some people across the room who had been to the same opening that they had. "Try the coquilles," he said to Iris. "They have a sweetness in France not like anywhere else in the world. They're very light, cooked in scallions and white wine."

"I'm sure they will be lovely," said Iris. "Is that—"

He interrupted. "Did I introduce you to those people? I meant to. He's a sculptor, nasty, but his work is good. And that's his wife. They have two identical twins, girls, 14, who are a little scary-looking. And they live in a stone house outside of Paris that used to be a mill. It's very beautiful. I want to show you—everything. I want to take you to the Pyramids. I want to float down the Nile with you. Don't laugh at me. I know, I would look funny floating down the Nile. I want to take you to the flea market in Nice and fall in love with a screen for the living room and bring it home."

"Is that what you wanted to tell me?" asked Iris.

"No, there's something I haven't told you. I meant to. There hasn't been an opportunity..."

The waiter arrived at their table with a 20-year-old bottle of Chablis. Maurice sampled it, discerningly, as if he was accustomed to returning wine, and then endorsed it. "Yes, that white wine would be lovely. Merci. See, I'm starting to sound like you." And then, to the waiter again, "We'll wait to order, thank you."

Iris wondered if it was possible to love someone more than she loved him. The white wine was chilled and so light it tasted almost like water from a mountain stream. But there was something that he wanted to tell her. And she knew from his tone, it might not be something she wanted to hear.

"I ought to have told you before. I am—" He

hesitated. "I feel as if we are in a glass bubble and I am about to shatter it. Don't let me." He took a sip of his wine. The words came out haltingly. "I am—I should have told you before— I am— I have—a wife."

Iris turned away from him, not knowing how to respond.

"Should I tell you," he said, "for many years we've lived as friends? It would not be the truth. But I will tell you that for many years, I've dreamt about finding you. Believe that. Should I tell you that we have an arrangement? It would not be true. And you are not the kind of girl who would go along with that. I will tell you, for many years, I have felt a sadness. And, now that I've met you, I would not know how to let you go. Please, believe that."

She had the feeling he'd rehearsed this, gone over in his mind what he was to say to her. And it softened it for her, made her listen more closely to what was to come. But Mary had been right. What did they know about him? Certainly not that he was married and, as he went on to explain, had two sons—17 and 14. She wished the wine was stronger.

"I ask you only for a little time, my love," he said. "Not much. There is no easy way to end a marriage. No good time to pick. I will not wait. As long as I know that you are waiting for me."

"You lied to me," said Iris. "I know you didn't mean to but you did. All of it was a lie except perhaps how we felt about one another."

"Buttercup..."

"Don't call me that. You have no right to ask me anything. We will see what you will do. You will forgive me, Maurice, if I don't stay for dinner."

He rose from his chair as quickly as she did.

"No, don't come with me. My French is good enough to hail a taxi."

And with a strength she didn't know she had, she

managed to leave the restaurant and walk half the length of the Champs Élysées before she started crying.

"I didn't tell you because I was so afraid that I would lose you. Have I strayed before? Yes, but never with my heart. I just ask for a little time, Buttercup. So that I can make it right."

She hadn't answered him. It didn't seem the sort of thing one could negotiate. Or on what terms. He would do what he did. And she would see how she felt when he did it. "Remember that I love you." Those were the last words he'd said to her, as she was leaving. And she would, always remember that he'd loved her, no matter what the outcome.

The ferry was making a slow approach to the little island that was their destination. Iris bit her lower lip and tried to maintain her composure. She was embarrassed. She had fallen in love with a married man. Of course, she had. No one had ever seen fit to be her suitor before. She couldn't tell them.

Mary would look at her knowingly since she had predicted it or predicted something, even if she didn't know what she was predicting. Or worse, she would pity her, suggest she go out and have her hair cut shear to the chin like Louise Brooks. Maurice had loved her for who she was. Iris Ogleby of the New York Oglebys. Her father had a company that sold copper pipes. They weren't artistic or intellectual. And until Maurice, no one had ever thought there was anything extraordinary about her. She was popular. But part of why she was popular was because she was available, sometimes an afterthought or a stand-in. She had to admit, she'd had a fantasy. And the fantasy went like this, that someone would love her and she would be the one who was giving the party.

I t looks like a natural lake," said Betsy Owen, as the ferry boat pulled up to the slip of an island that was their destination and the expanse of lake was visible behind them. "But it isn't. Napoleon III built it as a backdrop for his hunting lodge. Or maybe that's the falls, I can't remember. But he did build it. It's not even a lake-bed, it's poured concrete. And the water comes from artesian wells. Can you imagine?"

Iris couldn't imagine anything if Maurice wasn't with her. As the engine was silenced and the ferry boat came to a stop with a jolt at the small dock, she blurted out, "He's married!"

Betsy Owen and Mary just stared at her, at first, as if they couldn't believe what they were hearing.

"Married? I knew there was something wrong with him. I could tell from the first. Have you known—all along?" asked Mary as she stepped agilely from the boat.

"No, he told me last night at dinner."

"Was that all he told you?"

"No, he said a great many things..."

All of the other passengers had disembarked and Iris just sat there on the wooden bench of the boat, as if she had no intention of moving. "He told me," she said, "he had—has two sons." A line of people had formed who were waiting to board the ferry but Iris just sat on the bench of the ferry boat, oblivious that she was taking up their time. "He told me he was leaving his wife."

"Did you believe him?" asked Mary.

"I don't know."

The boatswain walked over to them, muttering under his breath, "Ah, ces maudits Américains, ils pensent que le monde peut s'arrêter pour eux," quite under his breath (although Mary heard him), as a polite translation would be, *Damn Americans, they think the world will stop for them.* And to Iris, he said, crisply, in English, "Do you wish to go back to the other side?"

"No, no, of course not," Mary answered for her curtly. "Come along, now," she said to Iris, softly, as if she was speaking to a child. "It's time to get off the boat. We'll have a lovely lunch and you'll feel better."

"Please, don't—"

"I'm sorry, I didn't mean to say that."

Iris stood, looking like a wooden doll who had been sprinkled with the powder of life, and awkwardly stepped onto the small wharf. "I don't expect I ever will feel better," she said, mournfully. In the distance, the bonnets of white and green umbrellas were visible from the patio of Chalet des Îles, jauntily tipped at angles to keep the sun off the diners. Maurice would agree with her that each had a distinct personality and wouldn't think it odd that she anthropomorphized an umbrella. She wouldn't think about him. They would have a lovely lunch and she would order duck confit. But in her mind, she heard him say, "Have the coquilles. They have a sweetness in France not like anywhere else in the world."

When they returned to the hotel, the concierge said to Iris, "These arrived for you, Miss Ogleby," gesturing to a dozen long-stemmed white roses arranged in a vase.

"Please, have them returned to Mr. Chabon at his gallery," she said immediately. She wrote the address down on a slip of paper. She did not open the card that was propped up in the stems. "I'll pay whatever the expense," she said curtly.

"Don't you even want to read the note?" asked

Mary. The gesture had surprised her, that Iris could be so competent and self-assured.

"No, not really," said Iris. "If he has anything to tell me, he can come and see me. And, until then, he has no right to court me. Thank you. I didn't think talking about it would make me feel better but I feel so much better since I've talked about it."

It was the first time in her life Iris had ever tried to put up a front except when her sister Essie was hospitalized with pneumonia and her mother was so upset that she didn't think her being upset would do any good. She marveled at how easy it was, how no one really knew what you were thinking if you didn't let them.

"Where are we going to have dinner?" she asked.

"Iris, we just had lunch."

"I know," she said, "but I'm afraid being single has made me hungry."

lara and Billy Holmes were waiting for them in the bar. Clara looked, there wasn't any other word for it, chic. She was wearing a burgundy suit with slightly ruffled sleeves and a white silk blouse underneath that was definitely French. She had bobbed her hair to accentuate its natural wave. She wasn't pretty. No, no one would ever say that she was pretty. But she was striking and Billy's taste, because they all assumed that it was Billy who had picked her clothes, was impeccable.

Billy was drinking scotch, even though it was four in the afternoon, and Clara was nursing a gin and tonic. She had a Piaget watch on her right wrist that Billy had picked up for her at an antique store. It had a simple black band and a plain gold rim around its face so that the numbers themselves were the set-piece, distinctly Piaget. Billy's linen suit was appropriately wrinkled. It occurred to Mary that they fit into Paris in a way that she never would.

Billy and Clara had arrived from St. Tropez by train early in the morning and spent the day shopping in Paris. They wanted a small nap and, then, Billy wanted them all to make a night of it, have a late supper at Le Petit Zinc and go to some of the jazz clubs in the Latin Quarter. It wasn't just Billy's desire to keep his finger on the pulse, to be involved in the latest happening even before it was a noted craze, it was as if he was endemically drawn to the center or the cutting edge, although often those two things were one and the same. Mary wondered if they had experienced Paris, at all, before Billy and Clara arrived.

"Billy, would you mind?" asked Clara. "I'm not really tired. Mary, would you come and have a walk with me, we could look in shop windows or walk along the Seine."

Mary wanted to go upstairs and see if Geoffrey Rice had returned yet. She was dying to tell him about Iris. She had walked along the Seine at five that morning and then gone to the island in the Bois de Boulogne. She was tired. But there was something about the way Clara asked, as if she needed someone to talk to. And, most likely, she did, she hadn't spoken to anyone except Billy since the wedding. And there must be so many things she wanted to say. "Of course, I would," said Mary.

Clara didn't say anything of substance for the first block, asking about the patisserie on the corner and if Mary had tried the chocolate shop—she had, of course—and if she had ever had absinthe?

"No," said Mary, "have you?"

"Billy made me try it in Marseilles," said Clara.

"And?"

"And—he isn't—constant," she said, jumping ahead to what was really on her mind. "That's the word I would use—constant. It's one thing when we're in New York and we're living our separate lives, but—I don't know where he is some of the time. The first time it happened, we were in Marseilles. It was the same night he made me try the absinthe. I awoke in the middle of the night and he was gone. I was so frightened. I didn't know anyone in the city. I thought, at first, he might have gone out for some air but when he didn't return in an hour and then three hours went by...and then five... I imagined the most terrible things. And, when he returned, he was so strange. He told me he'd spent the night walking, just walking, the streets, trying to quiet his mind. I believed him. I'd had an absinthe and he'd had three. I sort of believed him.

"We'd had a perfectly lovely evening. It seemed as if it came out of nowhere. We'd had dinner, a local fish soup, at a dive on the pier. We'd walked along the waterfront. It was warm out, humid, and smelled a bit stronger than it should, gamey. A French navy ship had docked and there were sailors on the wharf, some a little drunk, and it was an evening that I thought would be a memory. We stopped at a bar and had an absinthe. Even the color of it looks forbidden. I had trouble falling asleep. When I shut my eyes, I saw faces. It is a little hallucinogenic, I think. Not that I would know. But that's what it seemed like to me. And, finally, we both fell asleep. At least, I thought we had... It was a terrible night, made worse by the fact that I was feeling—altered. I didn't know where Billy was. I didn't know what had happened to him. I thought he'd left me.

"And, now, my sleep is always fitful. And, when I wake up and he's gone, it seems so unkind, as if he's punishing me. At first, that night in Marseilles, I believed him, that he'd needed to quiet his mind. In Monte Carlo, I believed him that he'd spent the night playing cards in a casino. And then, when it happened again in Nice, I believed him that he'd spent the night drinking in a café. But I don't believe that anymore. Do you think there's someone else?

Someone who he met in Marseilles? Someone who lives in Paris who met him in Marseilles—I imagine so many things. Do you think he stays up all night playing cards? Sometimes, he does drink too much..."

"Oh, Clara—"

"Don't say it. I feel so protective of him. I know you're right and everything you're about to say is right."

"Poor Clara."

"Yes, always, that's what they'll say about me. Poor Clara. And the terrible part is, in the daytime, we're perfect, as if nothing whatsoever had happened the night before."

J oe Zelli's was crowded, a haze of blue smoke and laughter hit them when they entered the room. Billy Holmes arranged, in a moment, to be on a first-name basis with Zelli and they were led to a table in the front of the room. He was attentive to Clara. There were pen-and-ink caricatures tacked onto the walls of French theatrical types, none of whom Mary recognized, except Maurice Chevalier. All the women were bare-armed, in skimpy tight-fitting dresses and impressive jewels.

Mary wondered if the peach slip of a dress she'd chosen made her look too *jeune fille*.

Zelli sent over a bottle of champagne. Iris wanted to know if that *was* Louise Brooks sitting at a table on the side. It looked like Louise Brooks.

"I could never look like that," she said to Mary. "Please, do not suggest to me that I cut my hair like her again. She's lovely. She's tiny and powerful and she draws men to her like a firefly."

"What makes you think that men are drawn to fireflies?" asked Geoffrey Rice, teasing her.

"You know what I mean," said Iris.

They had come to hear a black blues singer from New Orleans named Hutch but Billy must've got the nights confused. The entertainment that night was an aerial trapeze artist named Barbette who danced to a five-piece orchestra.

They were expecting a low-key night at a blues club and what they got was pure-theater, explosive, campy, and, at the end, a surprise, although Mary would wonder, later, if it was a surprise to Billy Holmes.

There were two French horns, a violinist, a trombonist, and a drummer. It was the French horns that announced her. The curtains parted and Barbette appeared, posed on top of a twelve-foot pedestal, wearing an enormous feathered headdress, a black choker with a diamond at its center, and an evening gown, with an elaborate sequined skirt, seven feet long, which sparkled and flowed onto the stage, concealing the base of the pedestal. Her make-up was theatrical, pale skin and heavily rouged cheeks, her eyebrows accentuated by kohl, the eyes themselves, lined and powdered, with eyelashes so long they had to be artificial.

To the strains of a Wagnerian melody, Barbette performed a pirouette on top of the pedestal and her skirt twirled and lifted to reveal the rest of the aerial ballet troupe, four male dancers, in bandolero pants and white shirts, posed underneath her skirt. As she stepped onto the high-wire, to a drum-roll, she performed a faux striptease, slipped out of her floor-length ballgown, and appeared in a tight-fitting leotard encrusted with jewels.

Swings, the ropes of which were braided with flowers, and gold rings dropped and were suspended from the ceiling and the four men swung Barbette and tossed her about as if she was a child. She performed jumps and flips and arabesques. She walked on her hands on the high-wire as easily as on her feet. And, in the end, she sauntered daintily off the trapeze, curtsied, changed her mind and bowed, and, in one gesture, removed her wig and revealed that she was really a man.

There was a standing ovation and the audience insisted with cries of *"Encore! Encore!"* on a reprise.

"There's a perfect French expression, *trompeuse apparence*," said Billy, clapping. "In art, it means false perspective. In life it means, not what it seems. Did you guess?" he asked. "I did. It was so theatrical and

I thought, even for a ballerina, her/his arms, calves were so strong, even for a dancer, and that little choker around his neck, it's always a complete give-away."

Mary wondered how much contact Billy had had with female impersonators. Certainly, more than she had.

As the lights dimmed again, Iris, who, now, could think of nothing but Maurice, how much he would have liked the show, how much she missed him, slipped out before any of the group could stop her.

"Do you think I should go after her?" Mary whispered to Geoffrey Rice.

"No," he answered, "I think she wants to be alone."

Now, that Barbette's illusion was dispelled, it was pure theater. The feather headdress was replaced by a feather boa and the dénouement was part aerial ballet, part circus-act, as two of the dancers held up an enormous ring and, to a drum-roll, lit it with a torch, and Barbette performed a backflip through the circle of flames. To applause and cheers, Barbette bowed, took off his wig again, flexed her/his arm, showing off his masculine muscle, and curtsied to the audience.

The curtain came down quietly. A small spotlight flashed on a piano at the foot of the stage, nothing flashy, just a little background music so that no one would think the night was over and that it was time to go home. The champagne was still flowing freely, a slip of a girl at the piano, her hair so short it was barely a cap on her head, in a wispy voice, was singing songs in French that could only be about love.

"I guessed, too," said Clara.

"Did you?" said Billy. "I'm not surprised."

"I didn't have a clue," said Mary. She felt as if everyone in the room was more sophisticated than she was, the blonde woman at the table next to them in a tight-fitting white dress, idly smoking a cigarette, Geoffrey, who could sometimes be so aloof and distant she felt she hardly knew him, Billy, lost in a haze of alcohol, his eyes shut, idly tapping his fingers in time to the music, Clara, who had made her own bargain with the modern world, the little slip of a girl at the piano whispering songs about love.

Mary looked over at Geoffrey Rice but his attention was drawn to the young woman at the piano, who was now singing, in English with a French accent, a Gershwin song, the words coming out in a whispered hush.

> *I'm a little lamb who's lost in the wood*
> *I know I could always be good*
> *To one who'll watch over me.*

As the singer continued in a wistful voice, Geoffrey said, "Isn't it strange how someone can whisper a song and have it be heard in the room."

Won't you tell him please
to put on some speed
Follow my lead, oh how I need
Someone to watch over me.

Mary wondered what it would be like to have that kind of allure, to simply whisper a song and have it be heard in the room.

Mary was the first of their party to come down for breakfast. It was after eleven and the dining room was almost empty. She sat at a table in the corner by the window. Her head felt like cotton. She'd had too much champagne the night before, too little sleep. She ordered a coffee and picked at a small baguette in the basket on the table. A light rain was falling and the city looked as if it was shrouded in gray.

A composed and immaculately dressed Clara Holmes arrived, soon after. She ordered two soft-boiled eggs and toast. There was something straightforward about Clara, unerring, uneventful, as if no matter what happened or what her mood, she would order soft-boiled eggs.

Mary asked if Billy would be joining them.

"No," said Clara, cryptically, "he stayed out much later, I'm afraid, than we did." She said no more except her meaning was quite clear.

Soon after, they were joined by a curiously quiet and content Iris Ogleby, seeming almost as if she had been sedated. Clara regaled them with stories about her and Billy's whirlwind trip. Mary listened politely to Clara's revisionist recounting of her travels abroad. Nice was fabulous. The antique stores weren't like anywhere else in the world. The small inn they'd stayed in at Provence had grown its own vegetables. She and Billy both agreed that they'd never experienced a tomato before. The port town of Marseilles was exotic and a little dangerous. Mary didn't really understand why any of it mattered if

Billy disappeared all night but she was too polite to mention it, since they were not alone.

But, then, Iris startled them both by placing her left hand on the table and displaying a diamond that quite took up the space between her knuckle and the base of her ring finger.

"When I came back to the hotel last night," she explained, breathlessly, "Maurice was waiting for me."

"And...?" asked Mary.

"And, he's left his wife. He asked me to marry him."

"And, you've accepted?"

"Yes, I would say I have." She laughed. "I don't know how I'll tell Mama and Papa. I thought you might help me, Mary. He wants to get married here, which, I think, under the circumstances, is a good idea. You know how people in New York like to talk and, as much as I don't mind giving them something to talk about, I'd rather not be there while they did it. Not that I care about a wedding. I'd be happy just to elope and go to Greece. I know—we can't get married until his divorce is final."

"And, until then?" asked Mary.

"Until then, I thought I'd stay here. Maurice is taking me to see an apartment this afternoon that he thinks might be good for us... Yes, I know. Don't look at me like that. Whoever thought that I would be living in sin? But hasn't anything ever just felt so right to you that you knew you had to do it?"

"And what will you do in Paris?" asked Clara cautiously, who certainly, from her vantage point, thought a whirlwind rush into marriage wasn't the best idea.

"I don't know," said Iris. "Whatever Maurice wants me to do. Become a patron of the opera, give parties, have lots of small children underfoot, most of them mine. I don't know. But whatever it is, I bet it will be lovely."

Betsy Owen joined them, soon after, walking with some difficulty, favoring her cane. She ordered tea sandwiches even though it was not yet noon and Iris had to tell the whole story all over again.

It reminded Mary of that Sunday morning, it seemed strange that it was only three months ago, that she and Betsy and Iris and Lucy had spent the morning playing cards. She wondered if her life would always be book-ended by four women sitting at a table with a view out the window of the street below. And if there would always be the shadow of Lizzie Carswell.

They had gone down the street and turned left. She remembered that. And, then gone one block or two. It all looked the same. Perhaps, if she walked all the way to the center of the Pont Neuf and retraced her steps... The farmers had been setting up for an open-air market. She remembered that. She wondered if the outdoor market was there every day or just on Saturdays.

And, then, there was the question of what she was going to say to the girl. She would ask how she was, she would, of course, do that. And try to get her to explain why she was in Paris. No, she would simply tell her to stop, immediately. It was different now that Clara and Billy were married. Certainly, even Lizzie Carswell would understand that. If, in fact, it had been Lizzie Carswell she had seen in the cathedral at Notre Dame and again, yesterday, in the open-air market buying apricots, and the curious thing she'd determined in the middle of the night—that Lizzie and Billy were still carrying on—had any merit other than in her mind.

Geoffrey had stepped into a patisserie and bought them coffees. If she could find the patisserie, she could retrace her steps from there. There it was, on the corner, a little blue-and-white-striped awning. No, that didn't look right. Perhaps it was another block along. Or was she walking on a parallel when she should be walking on a street that ran perpendicular to the Seine.

She turned and walked another block and then, two, and, there it was. The shop on the corner. That was where Geoffrey had bought the coffee and crois-sants. She had been standing across the street in the middle of the block. The open-air market wasn't there but there were still a few vacant pushcarts left as evidence on the sidewalk.

She was walking, slowly, studying the façades of the buildings, trying to determine which one she thought it was and she walked right into an old man whose jacket smelled like cherry pipe tobacco and reminded her, for a moment, of her father. Most likely, her father would tell her that she ought not to meddle.

The stone building was gray and architecturally unimposing but Mary hesitated at the door and re-alized, without quite knowing why, that she was frightened of the encounter she might have, as if she had a prescient notion that she might learn some-thing she did not want to know.

Should she be offering her assistance? Is that what she was supposed to do? If it was Lizzie

Carswell and she was alone in Paris, shouldn't Mary be offering her a hand? No, she was entitled to correct her. Lizzie was most likely feeling desperate and at-sea and not thinking straight in the least. If Mary offered her a hand while correcting her, Lizzie would see the error of her ways. She had to. But what if Lizzie was immutable? If it was Lizzie, after all?

Mary felt even more uneasy when she saw the name written atop one of the mailboxes, **No. 5 Carswell.** She had half expected she had gone on a fool's mission and, now, she was compelled to follow through.

The door wasn't locked. It squeaked a little on its hinges as it swung into the courtyard which wasn't shabby. It was not what she had expected, at all. It was as if the gray façade of the building was only there to camouflage the extraordinary garden inside. The walls were awash with sprays of flowers, the many stone urns brimming with blooms of their own, the stone benches inviting, the funny dragon's head that spilled water into a fountain, and the cherubic statue of a white angel holding a birdbath on its wing. Mary felt as though she was in the presence of what they call in New York "old money".

She walked up the stone stairway at the back of the courtyard that led up to *No. 5*.

She hesitated and then used the iron knocker molded in the design of a dragon's face. There wasn't any answer at first and then footsteps. And then, a young woman opened the door in a rush of French, "Oui, tout de suite...qui est ce? Une minute, attendez." She stopped speaking the moment she saw who was there. "Mary Nell," she said, matter of factly, as if she'd been expecting her, all along. She wasn't inviting or noticeably pleased to see her but neither was she surprised that Mary was there. "I suppose I should ask you in."

t wasn't elegant. No, no one would say that it was elegant. But it was tastefully decorated, each individual piece of furniture depicting a good eye and a careful hand. There was art, real art, on the walls and a beautiful Aubusson carpet, the floor lamps had tassles, and there were lots of silk throw pillows on the sofa. Mary wondered if this was the pied-à-terre of the people Lizzie had been sent to work for and if she had a narrow room somewhere off the kitchen and, any moment, there would be small children annoyingly underfoot. She would simply say what she had come to say and take her leave.

"It must be—terrible for you," said Mary, haltingly. She was about to ask how difficult it was to take care of small children in someone else's home, be sympathetic, when a very beautiful middle-aged woman appeared in the doorway. She was rail-thin and so delicate as to appear breakable. She had a long shock of dark hair that was pulled back severely into a French bun, accentuating her facial features. She had the sort of cheekbones that defy age and her eyes were so blue as to appear almost violet-colored, like Lizzie's.

"Mama, go back to bed... Yes, we have a visitor... An old friend of mine from school... You remember. Mary Nell."

"Yes, of course. Perhaps, the next time you're here, Mary, I'll feel better."

"Do you want me to help you, Mama?"

"No, Lizzie, I'm fine. It was nice to see you, dear," she said to Mary.

They heard her mother's footsteps down the hallway and the sound of her bedroom door close shut.

"She isn't well. The doctors say she may not get well," said Lizzie. "She had rheumatic fever when she was a child. I don't understand it, really. I don't want to understand it..."

"I'm so sorry," said Mary. "I didn't know."

"She's very cheerful about it. And I appreciate all the time I have with her. It's hard."

"Is that why you—left your job?"

"What—job?"

"Your father said that you had gone to Switzerland to work as an *au pair*?"

"Is that what he's telling people?"

"He said," said Mary, feeling bold, "he sent you off, after that night with Billy Holmes."

"I thought you'd seen us. I looked up in the

window and saw you watching me. I wondered what you thought. I thought you knew the truth, by now."

Lizzie's voice got faraway, as if she was telling something that had happened a long time before, and, in a way, it had. "Billy picked up a drifter," she said, "a boy who'd crashed his party. He said he was from a famous Philadelphia family but there wasn't any family by that name. The boy was—" she hesitated, as if looking for the right word, "—a poseur. I don't know what would have happened if I hadn't gone with them. I sent the boy home, at least, I thought I sent him home. I sent him away and stayed with Billy until he sobered up. We told the police all about it..."

"Told the police about it?"

"Yes, it was the same young man who washed up under the Hudson Street Pier. Billy had to identify him. They said it was a suicide. I thought you knew. The boy had a history with drugs or, at least, that's what the police thought after examining his body."

"Apparently," said Mary, "there are a great many things I didn't know." Her cheeks were flushed.

"Papa and I quarreled," said Lizzie, "but not about that. I wanted to come to Paris to look after Mama and he—he's never been able to forgive her. And so I left, without his blessing."

Mary felt she should apologize. She was about to offer some sort of request for forgiveness and whatever help she could—perhaps Lizzie did need money or, just, a friend—when she heard a man's voice in the entrance hall.

Lizzie had left the front door open and he bounded into the living room, "Darling, we should hurry. We're going to be late." It was Geoffrey Rice. And for some reason Mary couldn't fathom, not at first, he was calling Lizzie Carswell, darling.

"Mary—" He stopped when he saw her. "I didn't expect to see you."

"Nor I, you," she said. "Apparently, there are a great many things I didn't know. Will you excuse me," she said to Lizzie, "I need to be getting back."

She wouldn't cry. What was there to cry about? Had she misread so many signs? How solicitous he was of her, the way he stroked her hair in the middle of a conversation, how he thought nothing of waking her in the middle of the night if he needed a friend. That was it. He just thought of her as a friend. No. Friends didn't stroke your hair or touch your face in the middle of an idle conversation. Friends didn't kiss one another, did they? But had he kissed her? Not since they'd been in Paris.

She imagined it would only be a block before Geoffrey Rice caught up to her. That he would apologize, try to explain, perhaps, even, say it had all been a mistake. She would be elegant. At least, in front of him. But when she turned to look, he had not come after her.

She wondered what the others would say to her? If they would be sympathetic, suggest she cut her hair or buy a new dress, tell her she was better off? She didn't feel better off. Her cheeks felt like they were stinging, as if she had been slapped. To have misconceived so many things. It all had to do with— what was that expression Billy had used about the female impersonator—*trompeuse apparence,* which in art means false perspective and in life means, not what it seems.

She wondered if some people were meant to live life and others just to observe it. Was that the lesson she was supposed to learn? Was she supposed to make use of it? In a way, it was everything she had been looking for. It was like something in a story if you went back to that Sunday morning. People were always telling her to write what she knew. She would have to write about herself, of course, and the portrait would not be entirely flattering. And some of the others might mind, as well, but that was the nature of it. She would change the names. She would do that. She knew just how she would start it.

"She never did understand what it meant to be proper," *said Betsy Owen as she turned away from the window in a* *sweeping motion as though her skirt alone propelled her* *across the floor. And, there it was, in that one understated* *sentence, an indictment of all that Lizzie Carswell had ever* *hoped to be and an acknowledgement that there was a story* *behind the seemingly innocent act they had all witnessed.*